CRIME WAVE

A CANADA WEST ANTHOLOGY

Edited by J. E. BARNARD
Edited by KAREN L. ABRAHAMSON
Foreword by MELODIE CAMPBELL

Crime Wave

All rights reserved, including the right of reproduction, in whole or in part, in any form.

Published September 2020 by Sisters in Crime — Canada West Chapter

Copyright September 2020 Sisters in Crime — Canada West Chapter
Book and cover design © Sisters in Crime — Canada West Chapter

ISBN: 978-1-7772466-0-0

Copyrights to individual stories rest with the authors © 2020.

This book is licensed for your personal enjoyment only. All rights are reserved. This book is a work of fiction. Names, characters, places and incidents are the product of the authors' imagination or are used fictitiously. Any resemblance to actual events, locales or persons, living or dead, is coincidental. This book, or parts thereof, may not be reproduced in any form without permission.

If you purchase this book without a cover you should be aware that this book may have been stolen and reported as unsold and destroyed to the publisher. In such a case neither the author nor the publisher has received any payment for this stripped book.

For more information about Sisters in Crime — Canada West Chapter, please visit our website at www.sinc-cw.ca.

❦ Created with Vellum

CONTENTS

Foreword   v
From the Editors   vii

1. The Potluck Brigade   1
   By Alice Bienia
2. Local Intelligence   29
   By Debra Henry
3. Salty Dog Blues   57
   by Winona Kent
4. Cold Wave   91
   By Marcelle Dubé
5. News on the Buckhorn   111
   By K.L. Abrahamson
6. Autumn is a Time for Dying   133
   By Merrilee Robson
7. A Midwinter Night's Scream   145
   By J.E. Barnard
8. Pickled To Death   169
   by Charlotte Morganti

Acknowledgments   197
Author Biographies   199

FOREWORD

Crime has always been a woman's genre. Our most famous Golden Age authors were women: Agatha Christie, Dorothy Sayers and, in America, Mary Roberts Rinehart. They rocked the fair-play mystery, and were masters at building suspense. The authors in this anthology skillfully continue this tradition.

Why women and crime? Yes, we love a puzzle, and the challenge of pitting ourselves against the fictional sleuth. But it's more than that.

Real life doesn't always give us satisfactory endings. The good guys and gals don't always win. This brings me to justice, which I believe is at the heart of the genre.

In crime fiction, the murderer will be revealed at the end. Chaos will return to order. The western women featured in this anthology have brought that home. In typical western fashion, *justice will be done,* be it within the law or not.

The stories in this anthology cover the Canadian West, from past to present, from the Prairies to Vancouver Island, and north to the Yukon. They run the gamut from classic twisty mysteries to taut suspense, from stories with gravitas to those with humour.

A wild ride, as one would only expect of women from the west.

Melodie Campbell

FROM THE EDITORS

Editing the inaugural Canada West anthology has been a privilege and a pleasure. When we sent out our call for submissions for *Crime Wave* we wanted to represent the whole West — the territory of Canada from Saskatchewan westward. Most of our membership resides in BC's Lower Mainland, so imagine our delight when our 'wave' theme brought forth stories set from the prairies to Vancouver Island and all the way up to the Yukon.

A crime wave can be interpreted in many ways, but all of our stories build to a crest, in the crimes or in the stakes, or both.

In *The Potluck Brigade* visit a dying Alberta town and a senior citizen trying to cope with murder as well as her own failing mind.

The police procedural, *Local Intelligence,* follows a young RCMP constable in an isolated coastal town facing a most unusual collection of flotsam.

In *Salty Dog Blues* the crew and passengers on a west coast cruise ship confront a mystery involving a *verrry* annoying little passenger.

In the Yukon, *Cold Wave* forces a lone cross-country skier to choose between personal safety and saving her friends.

News on the Buckhorn brings us to central British Columbia in a taut suspense tale of a timid young girl dealing with the mutilation of her show horse.

Visit the prairies early in the Great War when a North West Mounted Police Officer investigates an unlamented death in *Autumn is a Time for Dying*.

An Okanagan bed and breakfast owner takes the stage in the rollicking *A Midwinter Night's Scream* to solve a tinsel-draped celebrity death.

Finally, in *Pickled to Death* a small BC town's annual Pickle Festival descends into chaos for a peck of unusual characters following the untimely demise of a perennial pickle aficionado.

So grab a coffee, find a comfortable chair and follow along with our investigators as they tackle the crime waves of the Canadian West.

J.E. Barnard and Karen L. Abrahamson

1

THE POTLUCK BRIGADE

BY ALICE BIENIA

Pulling her grey wool sweater tight against a cold prairie wind that knifed to the bone, Jan watched the gurney roll down the sidewalk. Sparse grasses, as dry and brittle as the hamlet's remaining inhabitants, quivered with each gust. Bleak, furrowed coulee walls stood fortress-like along both sides of the once bustling valley. Their shadows stretched long in the evening light, a grim reminder winter was on its way. Last year the snow arrived in late September, perhaps this year it would hold off a little longer.

The paramedics lifted the gurney into the waiting ambulance. A few grey wisps of hair escaped from beneath the sheet and lifted in the breeze. No need to hurry. No need for sirens or flashing lights on the return trip to Drumheller. Jan knew the body was a woman. She knew what had happened. She pulled out her phone and typed. *Gracie's dead.*

The door to the community centre banged shut behind Jan, the warm moist air inside a weird mix of disinfectant and dishcloths that should have been discarded weeks ago. Jan wiped her feet on the mat and crossed the foyer to the small storage room on the right, which also served as an office. She stuffed her hat into her coat pocket and hung it next to an old brown tweed coat. Muriel was already here. Muriel and Jan went way back, back to when their husbands were still alive and the coal mines were going strong. The town was different back then, full of hardworking men and women. Full of hope. Jan sat down on the bench, took her boots off and slipped on a pair of non-skid slippers. She smiled ruefully. For someone ready to meet her maker, she was being way too cautious.

She pulled a plastic container of roasted baby potatoes from her crocheted grocery bag and made her way into the main hall. Muriel rushed over, her right elbow arching backwards with every step, possibly an unconscious movement from the days she had to ward off all the men who wanted to sleep with her. Eighty-seven years of hard living hadn't fully erased the beauty with which she'd been gifted. Of course, her blonde hair was white now and the curls she once wore to the middle of her back were chopped into short waves, which from the back made her head look like a Chinese cabbage. Or maybe it was called an Asian cabbage now.

"Let me take these." Muriel reached for the container. "I'll get them on the table, then we'll eat."

Jan scanned the room. Roger had Alda cornered by the water cooler. She could tell by the expression on Alda's face that Roger was describing, for yet the hundredth time, how he'd been the first to spot the Little Blue Heron in Alberta. A sighting that earned him recognition by the North American Birding Association. A fact he'd never let any of them forget.

Muriel rang a small bell. "Okay, everyone. Let's eat."

They had been meeting twice a month for six years now. There were seventeen of them back then, now there were eight. The potluck had been Muriel's idea. Jan wasn't surprised. Muriel's Hutterite upbringing had burned the need for community dinner into her very DNA. That and an aversion to headscarves.

Jan hung back until only she and Bill were left. Bill waved her ahead.

"How are you doing, Bill?"

Bill grunted. "Hangin' in there. Damn snow seems to come earlier every year and stay later. Not good for my arthritis." The line stalled. Victor was holding things up, rearranging his plate so he could pile more on. "Did you hear Alda's son-in-law, Jack, applied for a development permit? If he gets it, he's going to turn the whole south riverbank into some sort of godawful tourist trap."

"Can't stand in the way of progress, I suppose. Only sixty-seven of us left, according to the last census and not many new folks moving in. We're pretty much a ghost town."

Bill snorted. "Doesn't mean we don't have an opinion on things. Guess that's what comes from being amalgamated with Drumheller now. Damn town council doesn't care what us old timers think."

Jan looked down at her plate. She'd been gabbing and had taken way more than she meant to. She wondered if she had any Alka-Seltzer left at home.

As soon as dinner was finished, Jan went to the storage room, opened the file cabinet and extracted a small black bag, several sheets of paper and scissors. She brought everything back to the table, now cleared of food. Bea was busily packing up leftovers to send home with whoever needed them the most.

Victor and Ruth were the usual recipients, although Victor had enough fat on him to last a whole winter.

Jan grabbed a sheet of paper and cut it into squares. She folded each square in the middle then folded it over again. Muriel joined her.

"Here's the bag," Jan pushed the canvas scrabble bag toward her.

Muriel counted out seven squares from the pile Jan cut and put them into the bag.

"Okay, we're ready," Jan called out. She turned to Muriel. "Who selects this time?"

"I picked last time. That means Rog goes next. His birthday's in March."

"Muriel, you've got the key to the box," reminded Jan.

"Oh, right." Clutching the bag, Muriel hurried out to the storage room. She returned a few minutes later, the bag in one hand, a wooden box in the other. She carried both over to Roger.

"Okay Rog, time to select a name. The blanks are already in the bag." Muriel unlocked the box, gave it a few shakes and held it over Roger's head.

The box held each of their names, placed there last April. On selection day, usually the first potluck of the month, one of their names was selected from the box and added to the scrabble bag, along with as many blank slips of paper as needed so that there would be one slip of paper for each of them.

Roger reached up and swirled his hand around in the box. He grabbed a paper square and added it to the blanks already in the bag. Roger shook the bag and passed it to his left. Bill pulled out a square and tucked it into his shirt pocket without unfolding it. The room was silent as the bag made its way around the table.

Jan wondered if she would pull a name or a blank this time. Her fingers scrambled against the cloth until they closed in on a scrap of paper. She pulled it out and stuck it into her sweater pocket. There'd be time enough to look later. She passed the bag with the remaining slip of paper back to Roger who, after extracting it, announced, "All done."

Another one of them had just been selected to die.

Donning her coat, Jan looked for Muriel. Ruth and Bea were giving the tables one last needless swipe, but Muriel was nowhere to be seen. It was unlike Muriel not to stay to the bitter end. Jan pulled her hat over her ears and stepped outside.

She heard herself huffing as she crossed the street. Leaving the last of the pavement behind, she slowed. A poorly lit lane led toward the sagging, crumbling shell that was her home. Once a happy place filled with children's laughter and warm cozy nights, the growing cracks and ever-increasing frigid winter winds swept away any desire to remain there much longer. It took more of an effort each time she left the house. Soon she wouldn't be leaving at all. She reached a fork in the path. After a moment's hesitation she turned in the direction of the river.

Dry brittle leaves crunched under her feet as she wove unsteadily down the winding trail. What if her name had been selected tonight? Was she ready to go? She stopped. The water flowed dark today, almost black under the dreary skies. She stood for a moment, fascinated by its relentless pounding journey. The river frightened her. She had always cautioned her children to stay away. She watched a snowflake drift downward, kiss the water and disappear. Then another, and more still. The flakes multiplied, over and over. She looked up. A shape, barely visible through the thickening whiteness, stood on the opposite bank. Watching.

Jan shifted her legs to the edge of the bed and waited until the vertigo stopped. She shivered and glanced at the warm jumble of blankets behind her. As tempting as it would be to crawl back under the covers, she'd already lain awake for an hour and her back was killing her. She rubbed some of the stiffness out of her hands and slowly stood up.

A sharp whistle jarred her to attention. How long had she been standing there? The kitchen was still frigid, but a fire burned in the old wood stove. Jan didn't remember putting wood in the stove or the kettle on for tea. But she must have.

Someone pounded on her door.

"Jan, Jan. Open up." The banging continued.

"I'm . . . c'm," her voice, dry and thick with sleep, stuck in her throat. She shuffled through kitchen and into the mudroom. A blast of cold swirled around her feet as she unlatched the back door. Muriel all but fell in.

"My god, what's wrong?"

"Victor's dead."

"Dead?"

"Ed found him. Went over this morning to sweep his sidewalk. Found him lying outside. The cops and ambulance are there now."

"What happened?" Jan asked.

"Jan, he didn't make it home last night. The leftovers were still laying next to him."

"You think a heart attack? It was bound to happen, with all that extra weight."

Muriel shook her head. "I went over when I heard the sirens. Jan, there's blood . . . blood everywhere."

"Here, take your coat off. I'll make you some tea."

Muriel's hands shook as she undid the buttons on her tweed coat.

"Leave your boots on," Jan said. "Florence is coming tomorrow to give the place a scrub."

"You know I can't do that. It'll just take me a second."

Jan shuffled back to the kitchen, pulled the kettle off the burner. She called out, "Have you eaten? I've got some crumpets."

She didn't get a reply. Muriel was in good shape for her age, but she was going deaf. Not that she'd ever admit it.

Jan took two mugs out of the cupboard and touched the faded words on one. *No matter how hard life gets at least you don't have ugly children.* A gift from her daughters on her 75th birthday.

"I've never seen so much blood, Jan." Muriel said, coming into the kitchen and closing the door to the mudroom behind her.

"Blood has a way of making it look worse than it is. I remember when my Jim cut his finger off with the band saw. I was sure he was going to die. Turned out he didn't even need a transfusion. You think Victor slipped on the ice, cracked his head open?"

"I don't know, Jan. It was a lot of blood."

"You can't think it was Victor that got selected last night. Hardly seems fair if it was." Jan vaguely remembered looking at the paper she had pulled, after she got home last night. She'd drawn a blank. Or was that the time before? She shook her head and placed a tea bag in each mug. Her mind wandered back to her girls. She wouldn't see them this Christmas. They were busy with their own lives, and she no longer travelled. It would have been nice to have a son around to help out with things. A big strapping fellow like that Jack Hofer. He reminded her of her Jim. Jan sighed. She really needn't refer to her husband as her Jim anymore. All the Jims in town had died or left years ago. Muriel was still talking.

"And to think he might have laid there in the cold, maybe for hours before he . . . before he . . . ."

"Died." Jan supplied, pulling the crumpets out of the toaster. She set a cup in front of Muriel and poured boiling water over the tea bag inside. She didn't know Victor as well as the others, but it was still sad to think he might be gone. If his name hadn't been selected last night, it meant two of them would be gone by the end of November.

They were just finishing their tea when Jan's phone rang. She rolled her eyes. "It's Rog."

"I'm calling an emergency meeting," said Rog.

"Why? What's happening? Is this about Victor?" Jan asked.

"Cops all over the place. We'll discuss it tomorrow — 10:30. At the community hall." The connection went dead.

"What did he say?"

"He's called a meeting. Tomorrow, at 10:30."

"I'm worried, Jan. What if it wasn't an accident? What if the cops know something?"

"Don't worry. You know Rog — Mr. 'I told you so.' He's always looking for a way to make himself look important."

After Muriel left, Jan pulled her sweater off the hook hanging next to her coat in the mudroom. She checked one pocket, then the other. Jan unfolded the square of paper she pulled last night and stared. *Victor.*

This morning, the coulee walls loomed dark against the flat grey sky, the gullies white with last night's snow. Glad she had remembered to bring her cane, Jan paused to catch her breath. She shook her head as she stared at the Wiesners' place. The windows were boarded up, the roof had caved in two winters ago. Now every second house was starting to look like the Wiesners'. Gone were the families, the children, the businesses. Only old folks now.

Jan was the last to arrive. Roger and the others were seated at two tables along the back wall. Soon one table would do. Bea was talking as Jan got to the table.

"This isn't what I signed up for. It's sick. And none of you figured it might not be a good idea to raise the cops' attention?"

Jan sat. "What do you mean? What's wrong?"

Bea turned to Jan. "No one deserves to die like that."

"Like what?" Jan looked around the table. Ruth adjusted the small tube running from the wheeled cylinder beside her to her nose.

"Gutted like some pig," hissed Bea.

"I thought he fell and hit his head on the pavement," Bill said.

"You wish." Bea leaned forward. "He was eviscerated."

"How do you know that?" asked Ruth as Alda clamped a hand over her mouth, stifling a small cry.

"Evan's youngest is a paramedic. He stuffed what was left of Victor into a body bag."

"A bit premature to be using the term eviscerated, Bea." Roger said.

Bea glared. "His intestines were all over the place."

Roger cleared his throat. "Regardless. We have a problem. The cops are looking into it."

"You can't believe one of us did this." Alda's eyes, round with fear, swept around the table.

"Keep your voices down." Roger admonished, nodding toward the far side of the room, where Ed, the community hall custodian, was taking down a Happy Thanksgiving banner. "I find it hard to believe a random stranger did this, the very night we selected a name."

"But we don't know Victor's name was selected." Jan protested. "It could have been any one of our names on that paper." Victor's name had been selected. According to the slip of paper in her sweater pocket, she had selected it. But given the circumstances, she didn't think it was a good idea to say so.

Roger cleared his throat and managed to look reticent. "The

paper I pulled out of the box last night wasn't folded tightly. The name started with a V."

"That's not fair," Bea protested. "We said we wouldn't reveal who was next. It's why we keep the box locked."

"Don't blame me. The paper wasn't folded tight. Not like I tried see whose name it was."

"Don't look at me," said Muriel. "I pulled a blank."

"Me too," said Rog.

"Stop." Jan turned to Roger. "It must be a coincidence. Besides," she felt her cheeks grow hot, "wouldn't it take a lot of strength to . . . you know."

Heads swivelled as the group took stock of one another. The coffee mug in Bea's hands continued to shake despite it being clutched with both hands. Alda still wore a tensor bandage on her wrist, broken in a nasty fall this past spring. Ruth would start wheezing the minute she unplugged from her oxygen tank.

"It gets worse." The silence stretched while Roger smoothed down his white mustache. "Gracie's son is demanding an autopsy."

Jan gasped. "But she's already been buried."

"He wants her exhumed."

"Holy Mother of Jesus." Alda made the sign of the cross.

"Why?" Jan asked, her heart jumping to an alarming rate.

"Apparently Gracie sent him a letter — telling him the town was expropriating her house."

"Well, I imagine she'd want him to know," Muriel said. "He's her only child and the executor of her will."

"We all know how Gracie felt about it," said Bea. "She made it clear at the town council meeting in June. Said she didn't care what they did after she died but she wasn't going to budge as long as she still had breath."

Ruth lifted her palms up. "I don't get it. Are you saying Gracie was killed so the town could get her land without a fight? What's that got to do with Victor?"

"Victor was opposed to the expropriation and the development permit Jack Hofer applied for to turn the south side of the river into some sort of theme park. You think it's a coincidence, that the two people standing in his way are now dead?" Roger snorted.

"What are you saying?" Alda's eyes widened.

"That's ridiculous," Muriel bristled.

"So what if the cops investigate Victor's murder. They won't find anything pointing back to us." Jan said confidently. If she had Victor's name, and she hadn't killed him, then clearly someone outside the group had.

All eyes turned to her. Had she just given herself away?

"I might have to agree with you on that one, Jan." Roger said. "The short cop? Dale? He's not exactly the sharpest tool in the shed."

Muriel winced at Roger's choice of words. "We have to stick together. We can't say a word about what we're doing. Not that it's so bad, it's just other people won't see it that way."

"I think we should cancel next month's selection," said Bill. "Wait for the dust to settle."

Bea's coffee cup clattered as she set it on the table. Without the cup to hold on to her hands jumped erratically. "My doc wants me in a nursing home. Since we agreed there'd be no selection in December, that would mean the earliest we'd select again is January."

Jan felt for Bea. Too bad Gracie had been selected before her, and Patricia before that. It was the only flaw in the process. The weakest weren't always the first to go. But selecting randomly was the only way to make it fair. Jan reached over and put her hand over Bea's, which fluttered under her fingers like a wounded bird.

"Let's take a vote," Jan offered.

Quietly their voices registered one by one. "I'm in, let's keep going, not backing out now…"

"Okay that's settled," said Ruth. "We select in November as planned. But no more violence. Agreed?" Everyone nodded. "Next potluck falls a few days before Halloween. Last chance to dress up."

Jan buttoned her coat as she made her way outside. She was pretty sure Bill was the one who had helped Patricia meet her maker. Bea had seen him leaving Patricia's house with a toolbox two days before she took a header down the basement stairs. Bill claimed Patricia had asked him over to fix a leaky faucet. But Jan had been over the very next day and Patricia had remarked on how well the faucet was holding out since her son-in-law repaired it last winter.

As far as Roger's theory went that Gracie's death was linked to her resistance to move off her land, that was pure nonsense. She had smothered Gracie to death with a pillow, herself.

"Jan? Jan? Wait up."

Jan turned as Muriel caught up. "Sorry Muriel. I just needed to get out of there."

"Are you okay?"

"I'm fine, just thinking. I don't think Victor was killed by one of us."

"You don't?"

"Bea's right. Why would any of us want to make Victor's death look like an obvious murder?"

"So, you think it was just a coincidence?"

"Not necessarily."

Muriel shook her head. "I don't understand."

"What if someone's figured out what we're doing? Decided to take advantage of the situation to kill Victor himself?"

"Why would anyone want to kill Victor?"

"That's where Rog's theory makes some sense. Maybe Jack doesn't want any more delays in getting his development permit approved. Even though Gracie's gone, Victor might have continued to cause a stink."

"Jack's lived here for years. I can't see him killing anyone." Muriel walked along silently for a few minutes. "What about creepy Ed? The way he mops the same spot twenty times, you just know he's listening."

"Ed's not creepy, just different. I doubt he knows what we're doing."

"Rog is in pretty good shape. He's not thrilled about Jack's development plans either."

"That's true. But if he killed Victor, would he admit he knew Victor's name was pulled? Besides he said he pulled a blank." They resumed walking. "I saw someone, Muriel, after our dinner." Jan shuddered. "Maybe the killer."

"Oh my god. Where?"

"On the other side of the river. I went down there on my way home to see . . . well you know, to look at the river. He was on the other side. Just standing there, like he was waiting for someone or watching for someone to get home."

"Did you recognize who it was?"

"No. It was snowing too heavily."

"What should we do?"

"Nothing. The group voted. We wait and select again in November."

Jan and Muriel parted where the pavement ended. Muriel's house was on the other side of the tracks. Jan continued down the uneven path, glad she had her cane with her. She limped past the front door and around to the back. It had been years since she'd used the front door, swollen shut from too much damp and too many layers of paint.

As she stepped in and bent to unzip her boots, she noticed it. A small square of paper under the bench, wedged halfway under the baseboard. She swiped at it, but her gnarled fingers couldn't quite get a grip. Boots off, she hobbled into the kitchen and got out a fork. One hand on the bench to steady herself, she knelt and stabbed at the paper, dragging the fork toward her. The paper slid out on the third try. Jan wiped a hand across her forehead, damp from the exertion. She struggled to her feet and slowly unfolded the paper. For one brief second her brain froze.

She staggered into the bedroom. Her hands felt along the bedspread, looking for the paper she had pulled. She stepped back, checked the floor. She'd taken it out of her sweater pocket yesterday and put it somewhere. Somewhere safe. She lifted a vase of artificial peonies off the dresser. Then the jewellery box. Two slips of paper lay there. She laid the square she had just found next to the other two. They looked like they came from the same stock. Hands trembling, she unfolded the squares. *Gracie. Victor. Gracie.* This couldn't be right. How could Gracie's name be on two slips of paper? Hands trembling, Jan scooped up all three bits of paper and made her way back to the kitchen. She yanked open the wood stove door, threw the papers in and added another stick of wood. She watched the papers curl until the flames licked up the last of them.

Jan didn't sleep a wink that night. Her mind puzzled over how a second piece of paper, with Gracie's name on it, had ended up in her house. She knew she was having trouble remembering things. Could she be sleepwalking? Doing things in her sleep she didn't later remember?

Last winter had been particularly brutal, with minus double-digit temperatures running forty-two days straight. When they finally got together, the talk had turned to how difficult surviving had become. Victor fell three times and had to call 911 each time for help. Ruth made it through the winter eating breakfast bars and peanut butter, which left her skeleton thin. Jan was too embarrassed to mention she'd lost command of her bowels. They all knew it was only going to get worse.

"I want to go out with some scrap of dignity." Jan had declared. That was quickly echoed by the others.

"What about medically assisted death?" Ruth had asked.

"Death needs to be imminent. I still don't qualify," Bea had replied. "By the time I do, I won't be able to make the request."

"I suppose there's always suicide." Roger had offered.

"Suicide will invalidate my life insurance, that's all I have to leave my son, and he's struggling," said Bill.

Other objections followed — the stigma that came with suicide, the fear of only partially succeeding.

"What if we killed each other?" Jan offered.

They had discussed the idea over several months. Finally, the rules were set. They put their names into the wooden box. On a selection month, a name would be picked randomly and placed in the black bag. Whoever picked a paper with a name on it had to terminate that person before the next selection. It was possible to have to kill more than once. And if one pulled their own name, which hadn't yet happened, they could call a do-over. Or kill themselves.

Jan assumed the game was being played by the rules they set, of which there weren't many. The longer she thought about things, the more convinced she grew that the rules were being broken. She hoped it wasn't her that was breaking the rules. More likely, someone else had joined their unofficial murder club.

The next week, Jan made the first of several trips into Drumheller. At city hall she read the town council meeting notes and studied the development permits.

Jack Hofer had been buying up land around town. He had purchased the old hotel and was planning to rent out theme rooms. Jan had no idea why people would pay more to sleep in a bed made from an old coal car, but apparently, they did. Jack now owned all the land south of the river, stretching from the old trestle bridge down to the slag piles west of the tipple. He planned to turn the old coal mine into a tourist attraction and the surrounding area into a theme park.

The old wooden trestle bridge could no longer support the anticipated traffic. The logical place for a new bridge was next to the old one. The approach required the land under Gracie's house. With the old crumbling neighborhood being a drain on town revenues, town council were eager to approve the development permit, which in turn meant expropriating Gracie's land. Gracie had refused to budge. Victor had written to the town council, the newspapers and the local television station, vowing to stop the development which would bring noise and traffic to the area. And displace a senior from her home.

Jack wasn't a complete stranger, he had ties to the area. He was married to Alda's daughter, Megan. Megan had left the community to go to university but returned eight years ago with husband Jack in tow.

Jan wondered if the figure she saw across the river could have been Jack. It would have only taken minutes to cross the old trestle bridge to Victor's house. Had he been waiting, watching for Victor to get home, not her?

It was late by the time she left town hall on her third visit. She reached the corner and stopped. Jan looked back. Nothing looked familiar. *Where was she?* She must have gone the wrong way. She felt lightheaded, her throat tightened, her heart pounded in her chest. A car screeched to a stop as she stepped off the curb. Flustered, she stepped back.

"Are you all right, dear?"

A woman with a kindly face stood on the sidewalk. Jan knew she should answer but couldn't think of a word.

"It's Melanie. From the community centre. I teach the Yoga classes there."

"Yoga." Jan smiled, still with no idea who the woman was but glad she was able to utter something instead of standing there like a stupid cow.

"Here comes our bus. You are going home, aren't you?"

Jan climbed onto the bus, the woman behind her. Only once they got to the community hall did things start to look familiar.

Chilled to the bone by the time she got home, Jan hung up her coat and went straight in to stoke the fire in her little black stove. She stirred up the hot coals and threw in some kindling. This wasn't the first time she'd gotten lost. In fact, it was becoming a regular occurrence.

She set a pot on the stove and reached to pull open the drawer. Soup would be just the ticket to ward off the chill. "Jesuz mercy," she muttered. Jan jiggled the drawer hoping whatever jammed it would fall into place. She stretched her fingers through the opening but couldn't reach whatever was stuck. She clumped over to the stove, grabbed the poker and stabbed it into the drawer repeatedly. Getting no result, she pressed down with her whole weight. She heard a crack and the drawer sagged. Furious, she reached in, grasped the object, and wiggled it out. Jim's boning knife. The end was dark, coated in dried blood. How could he not have cleaned it after using it last?

The sweat on her forehead froze as a cold fear gripped her. She'd opened the drawer this morning, to get a spatula. The boning knife hadn't been there. The room tilted. The knife clattered to the floor.

Jan struggled out of her old green rocking chair. She must have fallen asleep. A scorched odour filled the air. She shuffled to the stove. The pot stood empty; the bottom blackened from the heat. Using a towel, she picked it up and dropped it into the sink. *How long had she been asleep?* She looked out the window. It was already dark. She'd had such a strange dream. She looked down as her foot nudged something.

Jan covered her mouth with the back of her hand and staggered back. Her heart hammered in her chest. It hadn't been a dream. She had selected Victor's name. She'd sliced him open with Jim's boning knife — the one he used to prepare and dry meat in the shed out back. She'd been having lapses in memory, losing track of time, getting lost. There was no other explanation.

At four in the morning Jan found herself at the river's edge. She had calmed down some, enough to think. She couldn't let them find her with Victor's murder weapon. It would kill her children.

She carried a flashlight in one hand and the boning knife, now wrapped tightly in newspaper, in the other. She reached the edge of the river and looked into the blackness. It lay calm tonight, hardly a ripple as it slid along, like a giant eel silently pulling everything in its way into its huge belly. For once she wasn't afraid.

She lifted the knife over her head and heaved as hard as she could. She listened for the splash but wasn't sure she heard one. She started to turn and froze. A small light bobbed across the river in among the willows and disappeared.

Jan didn't go to the potluck at the end of October, claiming she didn't feel well. She was glad they weren't selecting until next time. She needed time to think. Victor's and Gracie's deaths were all over the news. Gracie's body had been exhumed. Originally labelled as death from natural causes, the ME now believed Gracie Costello had been suffocated. Police were still looking for Victor's murder weapon, speculating it might be a meat hook or boning knife.

Jan looked up at her TV. The newswoman was talking to the

chief of police. With two murders occurring so closely together in the tiny community, Police Chief Monette was asked what he made of the recent crime wave.

Crime wave. Jan huffed. The real crime was watching folks around here struggle to heat their crumbling homes or buy enough to eat. The police chief spoke for several minutes saying little or nothing, but ended with assurances he and his team were doing everything they could to solve these baffling cases. Jan let out a deep breath. Maybe she didn't need to worry after all.

Something niggled at Jan's brain and disappeared before she could grasp it. Why could she remember smothering Gracie but couldn't recall killing Victor? Fearing she had killed Victor during one of her blackouts, she had carefully examined her clothes and shoes for blood but found none. But the bloodied murder weapon had been in her kitchen drawer. And she had pulled Victor's name from the box. Hadn't she? Then, there was that second slip of paper with Gracie's name on it. Her mind raced through all the ways that could have come about.

Muriel came to see Jan the day after the potluck, brimming with news.

"The cops took Ed down for questioning yesterday. Picked him up while he was buffing the hall floor."

"He can't possibly tell them anything," Jan said more confident than she felt.

"I heard he told the cops we have some sort of murder club going." Muriel said. "We decided that if the cops ask, we'll just say we pick a name each month and that person selects an unsolved murder for us to discuss at the next few potlucks."

"That's a good idea. What unsolved murder should we say we've been discussing?"

"Ruth suggested JonBenét Ramsey."

"Oh, that's a good one," Jan nodded. "I always wondered if her brother did it. So, did anyone hear if they found anything when they dug up poor Gracie?"

"Bea said there were fibres in her throat." Bea always had the latest scuttlebutt. It helped that half her family were either paramedics, police officers or firefighters. "They hauled bagsful of stuff from her house to test. Bea heard none of it matched. The fibres they found were mohair."

That evening Jan cut the mohair scarf she'd worn to Gracie's into pieces and burned them. She felt herself sliding into a dark place. It came each winter, had for years. They had a name for it now. Seasonal Affective Disorder. She had always called it the winter blues.

She started going down to the river more frequently. Muriel came by several times to see if she wanted to go to the winter market, but Jan declined. Seemed like every time she left the house, she either had a panic attack, forgot where she lived, or killed someone. Besides, the less she had to distract her, the more able she was to think

The police stopped by, wanting to know about the last time she saw Gracie. Jan told them she'd been to Gracie's for tea the very day she died. She'd made sure Gracie died on a Thursday since they always played cards on Thursday afternoon. That way if anyone saw her coming or going, suspicions wouldn't be raised. They asked about Victor too, making it clear they were interested in the fact that two people, both opposed to Jack's development, were now dead. Maybe it's why the cops let Ed go without charging him.

The more Jan thought about all the things that didn't add up, the more confident she grew someone wasn't playing fair. Jan was convinced that Victor's killer wanted the cops to investigate. She certainly wouldn't have wanted to bring that down on herself.

That was when Jan realized she wasn't completely losing her

mind. She was being framed. She started to think about who might want to see her take the fall for Victor's murder. Maybe all the murders.

Jan paid Alda a visit. She wanted to know more about Alda's son-in-law, Jack, where he'd grown up, how he met her daughter. He reminded her of her Jim back in the day, a kind man, nice looking too. During the visit, Alda told Jan she thought someone outside the group must have killed Victor. Bea had told her that she had pulled Victor's name but didn't kill him.

How could Bea have pulled Victor's name when Jan had? She left Alda's place convinced someone had taken over their selection process to suit their own needs.

After her visit with Alda, Jan visited Bea. Things started to fall into place. Jan grew more confident in her theory that Alda would be selected next. And that something would be left behind to point Alda's murder to Jan.

As Jan neared the community hall, she could see Ed had already spread salt. The little granules shone on the sidewalk, wet in the afternoon sun.

Jan entered the hall and scraped her boots on the thick mat by the door. A yoga class was underway in the main hall. Or it could be Pilates or Tai Chi for that matter. All she knew was her body didn't bend like that anymore.

She was early but suddenly worried it wasn't early enough. She hurried into the storage room and set the buns for tonight's potluck on the desk. She slid open the top file cabinet drawer. Roger would have the key to the box. The last person selecting, locked the box and kept the key until the next selection. She picked up the box and slipped a bobby pin from her hair. Four minutes later she had it open.

Seven folded squares lay against the velvet lining. Fingers

trembling Jan opened them one by one. All their names were there — except for Victor, Gracie, and Patricia of course. She refolded the papers, put them back in the box and locked it. Melanie came in while she still had the file drawer open, the class now over.

"Whew! What a workout. Jan, you're early today."

"I'm not — I mean I'm missing a glove. Thought I'd come early to look for it."

"This glove," she picked up the glove lying on top of the file cabinet.

Jan laughed in relief. "Yes. I can't believe I didn't see it lying right there."

"Happens to me too. I once spent ten minutes looking for my phone — found it in my hand."

By the time the others arrived, the table was covered with a paper tablecloth, the plates and napkins. Cutlery was neatly stacked at one end and the kettle was plugged in.

Keeping an eye out to make sure Ed wasn't lurking, they discussed the latest. After the national news ran the story about someone killing seniors in their community, the RCMP had been called in to help.

"We should stop," Ruth said. "At least until spring."

"We decided we'd continue," Muriel said. "But maybe this should be the last one for a while."

"If we do this," cautioned Bea, "it has to look like an accident or natural death, not like we're being victimized."

"Maybe we should provide whoever . . . you know . . . an alibi," Alda said.

"If that's the case," Roger blustered, "we might as well select in the open." As the discussion continued, the kettle started to shriek.

"I'll get it," Muriel offered, getting up. The disruption reminded them they were also here to eat. Conversations dwindled as they lined up to fill their plates.

Jan noticed Muriel had disappeared. A few minutes later Muriel stepped out of the storage room. She saw Jan watching her.

"Thought I left my cell phone in my coat," she said as she got into line behind Jan. "It's not there. Must have left it at home."

"Well, are we doing this or not?" Ruth asked once the food was packed away, the table cleared.

Heads nodded. Jan felt something she hadn't felt in years. Maybe she wasn't ready to go. Then she remembered the panic attacks, the times she'd been lost. She hadn't recognized her own neighbour.

Roger and Jan brought out all the materials. "I got here early," Jan said, "so took the liberty of cutting and folding up the blanks." She counted out loud as she put six squares of paper in the scrabble bag. Roger unlocked the wooden box that held their names. "Who picks?"

"That would be me," Bill replied. Roger shook the box. Bill reached up without fanfare, pulled out a slip and added it to the bag. The bag made its way around the table. As soon as they were finished, Roger handed the key to Bill so he could lock the box.

"Just a minute." Jan stood up, the sudden rise making her lightheaded. "I believe someone's tampered with the names in the box."

"That's crazy," replied Muriel as everyone glanced at each other.

"We'll see. If I guess what name Bill will pick out of the box next, will the rest of you listen to me?"

"What are you doing Jan? Have you lost your mind?" Muriel's eyes flashed. "Bill's already picked."

Roger looked around and frowned. "I say we let her. But keep it down folks," he nodded to end of the hall where Ed was balanced on a ladder, changing a lightbulb.

"Why not?" Ruth chimed in quietly. "I have no idea what's going on but it's not like we're selecting a name, we've already done that."

"I don't agree with this." Muriel hissed.

"Why not?" Jan challenged. That got everyone's attention. Jan got the nod from everyone but Muriel to go ahead.

"Okay Bill. The name you'll pick is Alda."

Alda made the sign of the cross. Muriel glared at Jan.

Bill plucked a piece of paper from the box. He unfolded it then turned it around for everyone to see. "Alda," he said.

"How did you know?" several chorused.

"I can do one better. If we pull another name from the box it will say Alda, too. So will the next one."

Alda looked confused. Roger grabbed the box, dumped the contents in front of him. Eager hands reached to help unfold the squares. Six slips of paper lay on the table, all labelled Alda.

"And mine makes seven." Ruth unfolded the one she had selected from the bag.

"What the hell is this," Roger demanded.

Muriel backed up.

"I can tell you," Jan said. "Jack spent a lot of money fixing up the old hotel. If he doesn't get the development permit, and the money he needs to build his tourist attraction, he'll go broke. All that was standing in his way was Gracie's land, the town council's approval and some much-needed funds. Alda holds the third key to what Jack needs. Money. Alda, everyone knows your daughter, Jack's wife, will inherit everything when you pass."

Alda gasped. "No. Jack's a good man. A good husband and father. He'd never be involved in anything like this. He'd never kill anyone."

"He doesn't know anything about this," Jan said. "He didn't kill anyone either. Muriel, why don't you explain."

"Okay, okay. But what does it matter? We all agreed to do this. If we carry on, not one of us will be alive by next fall. Does it matter who goes first or third or fifth?" Muriel glared defiantly at the group.

"Then why not let things play out like we agreed?" Bea said.

"Because Jan's right, Jack will be bankrupt before spring if he doesn't get things moving," Alda said.

"But that's not all, is it Muriel?" Jan turned to the group. "She set me up to take the fall for Victor's death. Save her own ass if it came to that. I pulled a blank last time or was pretty sure I did. But the next day I found a paper with Victor's name on it in my sweater, instead. I thought I was losing my mind. Last week Alda told me Bea had pulled Victor's name." All eyes swivelled to Bea.

"Sorry Bea, but we would have never known if you hadn't said anything. Muriel didn't care who pulled Victor's name. She killed him that very night, then planted a slip of paper with Victor's name on it in my house. Planted the murder weapon in my kitchen. She was counting on whoever pulled Victor's name to keep quiet after he was killed. Bea certainly did, at least for a while. I didn't say anything when I thought I might have actually pulled his name. For a while there, I even thought I killed him yet had no recall of it. She wanted me to think I was losing my mind."

"Forgive me, but I don't get it." Ruth turned to Muriel. "Why do you care what happens to Jack? Why would you want to frame Jan?" All eyes swung to Muriel. She took another step back, fingers clenched into a fist.

"I forgave you," Jan said. "I forgave you and my Jim. But you never forgave us, did you? You never forgave me for staying with Jim after I found out he cheated with you. And you never forgave Jim when he told you he'd never leave me. Even if you were pregnant."

Alda gasped, the room grew silent.

"I had to give him up. You all know what Otto was like. He would have killed me if he found out. Maybe Jim too."

"So that's why you came to see me," Alda said softly, looking at Jan. "Wanting to know what I knew about Jack, his birthday, where he grew up."

"When you told me he'd been adopted, raised by the Hutterites, it all made sense. You grew up in a Hutterite colony near Lethbridge, didn't you Muriel? Same as Jack. Then I remembered the summer after I caught you cheating with my Jim, you left town for a few months. Said your family was going through hard times and needed your help on the farm. When Jack showed up here, I couldn't help noticing how much he looked like my Jim. I even mentioned it to you, Muriel."

"Is this true?" Alda looked at Muriel. "Are you sure the baby you gave up is Jack?"

"Oh, for once, Alda, don't be so goddamn naive. I know the family who raised my baby, they were strict, hard people. My sister would send me news of Jack from time to time. He was always in trouble, fighting the rules, the life I threw him into. The life I was once so eager to escape, that I married a brute who knocked me around until the day he died. I knew Jack was mine all along."

Bea's mouth had been hanging open. "So, you killed Victor? Like that? You wanted Jan to take the blame?"

"That was just a little added touch. It was so easy. I had a duplicate key made after my turn to select and lock up the box. It didn't take long to empty our names and replace them with Victor's, like I did with Alda's tonight. Later, I put the remaining names back in. I just didn't know who would pull Victor's name or who would pull a blank. But it didn't matter, because I planned to beat them to the punch. And Jan's right, I knew whoever pulled Victor's name would be in no hurry to admit it."

"That's why I ended up with Gracie's name twice," Jan nodded. "She planted Gracie's and Victor's names in my house, along with Victor's murder weapon. But she didn't know I had pulled Gracie's name the month before. What were you planning to do Muriel? Tell the cops you thought I killed both of them?"

Bea turned to Muriel. "You killed Victor — like that? And tried to pin it on Jan? It's not her fault you had to give up your baby."

"I think it goes further." Roger turned to Muriel. "You were going to determine the order we all went in, until only you were left standing at the end."

"No, Rog. I just wanted to clear the way for Jack. Make things right for him. He was going bankrupt. It was the least I could do. The thing with Jan, well it was just insurance in case the cops caught on."

"Insurance, my ass. The way Victor was killed, it's clear you wanted the cops to come looking." Roger glared at Muriel.

"That was you across the river," exclaimed Jan, as the last piece of the puzzle clicked into place.

"Yes. I watched and waited until you went home, into the house. Then I took the boning knife from the shed and the extra key to your house." Muriel laughed. "I'll never forget your face when you told me you might have seen the killer."

"What do we do now?" Bea's hands fluttered in front of her. "We can't turn her in, not with what we've been doing."

"I call a do-over." Roger's face was flushed. "We re-select a name, then let it lay a while. Where are the original names, Muriel?"

"They're in the storage room, under the printer. I'll get them."

"No, I will." When Roger returned, he handed everyone their

original slips of paper back, including Alda. Everyone checked their name, refolded the square and dropped it into the box.

Jan swept the other bits of paper, all with Alda's name on them, into a pile. "I have more blanks, I cut extras, thinking this might happen." Jan hurried to the storage room and came back with slips of paper, already folded. She counted out six squares, placing each into the bag. "Ok we select again."

Alda crossed herself. Roger gave the box a shake, Bill reached up, pulled a name out and added it to the black bag. After all the slips of paper were extracted, Roger brought a pot over from the kitchen. He looked over at Ed, who had the ladder folded and was carrying it to the storage room. After Ed left the room, Roger swept the pile next to Jan into the pot, added the remaining names from the box, and lit them on fire. The papers curled and burned and when only ashes were left, Jan took the pot, washed the ash down the sink before Ed returned.

Jan wasn't surprised when Muriel was found dead three weeks later. A fisherman spotted her body in the river. Serendipity, everyone wondered. Karma, Bea had declared. Jan smiled as she remembered Muriel's words the night she confronted her. *"Does it really matter who goes first or third or fifth?"*

Turns out it did.

2

LOCAL INTELLIGENCE

BY DEBRA HENRY

A pale arm reached skyward from a tangled mass of bull kelp that rocked gently in the bay's dark, frothy waves. A body?

RCMP Constable Hazel Quinn set her binoculars onto the hood of the patrol car as Bob Corker, better known locally as Corky, stood twitching nervously on the sidewalk that hugged the waterfront in Turnaround Bay.

"I was on my way to the store for some groceries, just minding my own business, when I saw it . . . ." He swung his arms toward the mass of seaweed floating just offshore. "I think someone's drowned."

The tide was at its low point, leaving behind a long slick shoreline, so Constable Mark Connors, Hazel's partner, stepped down onto the bouldered beach and stumbled awkwardly over its treacherous surface. Hazel locked the patrol car and carefully followed.

Mark hesitated at the water's edge, took off his utility belt, boots and vest, then stepped into the cold, choppy surf. As he made his way precariously toward the floating debris, he slipped and fell. Hazel cringed while he tried desperately to regain his footing.

He came up quickly, stood and grasped a loose end of kelp, reeling it toward him. Gradually the entire mass reached shore and Mark emerged from the water, sopping wet.

"Are you okay?" she asked.

A frown appeared on his round brown face. "Don't ask," he said. His black hair was dripping wet, his uniform soaked.

Hazel pulled on a pair of latex gloves from her pocket. "Let's see what we're dealing with here."

They dragged the kelp onto the beach and began to untangle the corpse.

"Shit. It's a bloody mannequin, Corker!" Mark shouted as Corky made his way toward them. "You take us for suckers or something?"

Corky took his ball cap off and scratched his head. "You sure about that?"

Hazel had been posted in Turnaround Bay for four months. In that short time, she'd discovered Corky had a reputation for his oddball humour. Would he throw a mannequin into the bay as a joke, though? Maybe.

"Think we should call the coroner?" Corky asked, grinning.

"I don't think that'll be necessary," Mark said. He sat down, took his socks off and wrung them out.

Corky turned the mannequin over. "Wow. She's pretty well endowed. I wonder where she came from?"

Mark shrugged. "You got me there. Maybe she was out sightseeing and fell off a boat?"

"Come on, Mark, don't get him started," said Hazel.

"I don't recognize her as local," Corky went on. "I wonder if she's single."

A crowd had gathered on the sidewalk at the end of Kingfisher Lane. A few held cell phones pointed in their direction. "I'm not sure we have a crime here," Hazel said.

"Someone's obviously missing a mannequin. If we find out who it is, the best we can do is charge them with littering . . . or mischief." She glared at Corky who pulled his ball cap low over his eyes and shrugged.

"Well, I'll leave her in your capable hands," he said. "If you're planning to take her back to the detachment, I'd recommend dressing her first. Otherwise Sergeant Ferguson's liable to arrest her for indecent exposure." He wiggled his bushy eyebrows and cackled.

Hazel drove Mark home to dry off and returned to the detachment where she deposited the mannequin on the floor beside her desk. She filled out an incident report, then filed the paperwork for a 'drunk and disorderly.' Drinking. The cause of so many problems. Her fiancé, Liam, had been charged with a DUI six months ago in the Okanagan. It led to a collision that killed his passenger, one of Hazel's close friends.

After deciding to leave Liam behind, telling him she needed to get away from Penticton, she'd taken the first transfer offered: Turnaround Bay. Every time Liam phoned, trying to patch things up, temptation crept into her head. He said he'd gladly join her on Vancouver Island, but she wasn't sure she wanted him back into her life. Twisting the diamond engagement ring still on her finger, she let out a long sigh.

A call forwarded to her desk interrupted her thoughts. A woman on the other end of the line said she'd been kayaking north of town when she noticed what looked like a body. "It was caught up in some driftwood. I — I didn't want to go any closer," she said.

Hazel took down a few notes, grabbed the keys for the patrol car and left the office. Was she dealing with a dead body or another hoax? She'd soon find out.

A small group of people stood huddled together at Winston Beach. The kayaker who'd called the detachment fidgeted with her paddle as she pointed toward several logs on the beach.

"It's over there," she said, her face pinched and anxious.

Hazel scanned the area as noisy seagulls wheeled in the air. She asked onlookers to stay back while she strode toward the logs with the crime scene kit. She hesitated. Time in the water could do terrible things to a corpse. With her boots off and gloves on, she took a deep breath, waded into the waves and peered between several logs jutting out into surf.

The body lay wedged between some driftwood, face down in the water, legs stretched out into Broughton Strait. She grabbed the body and wrestled it free.

The kayaker gaped at the naked figure. "Oh my god, it's a mannequin!" she said. "I'm so sorry."

Someone whistled. "Six foot-two. He's quite a catch."

"You should take him in for questioning." someone else said. "Ask him if he's lost his way?" People began to laugh with relief.

Hazel smiled. "I'm not sure how much we'd get out of him." She scanned the group, searching for Corky. She'd definitely bring *him* in for questioning. Unfortunately, he was nowhere in sight.

As she dragged the figure toward the patrol car, her pant legs sopping, a man held up his phone for a photo. "I've heard the Mounties always get their man."

"You got that right," she said. Too bad Mark wasn't with her. He always had a good comeback when people got cheeky.

Once she was back in the office, Hazel set the male mannequin on the floor next to the female from

Kingfisher Lane, exchanged her wet slacks for a dry pair, then filled out another incident report.

"Shit, we've got two dummies on our hands now," Mark said when he came back into the office. "Where'd you find Mr. Big and Tall?"

Hazel rolled her eyes and explained. Before she could decide whether finding two mannequins on local beaches could be a coincidence, Mira, their receptionist, poked her head into the office.

"We just received a report about a body found floating near the government wharf. Apparently, it's a child . . . but hold your horses."

"Let me guess," Mark said. "Another mannequin?"

Hazel slumped back into her chair. "Just what are we dealing with here?"

Mark shrugged. "A family, maybe?"

Sergeant Ferguson was in a foul mood when he stormed into the detachment after an extended lunch, his grey mustache bristling.

"What the hell's going on?" he grumbled, eyeing the mannequins lying on the office floor. Ferguson had been posted in Turnaround Bay six years ago. Mark had warned her it was easier to work around him than with him, so she — and everyone else in town — put up with him while he reminisced about 'the good old days.'

Mark grinned. "They showed up on our beaches. I'm not sure if they're tourists or someone's idea of a practical joke."

"Sir," Hazel said, but Ferguson cut her off.

"We're a laughing stock," he snapped. "Just look at this." He passed Hazel his cell phone. She glanced at the screen. A Facebook photo of Mark holding the female mannequin on the beach showed him standing in his soggy uniform, one hand clamped over her breasts. A second photo, taken by an onlooker, recorded Hazel hefting the naked male mannequin in a chokehold after freeing him from the logjam. The final picture revealed a firefighter carefully holding the mannequin of a child with an ambulance and fire truck in the background. A caption underneath read: "Local first responders rescue drowning victims. Which ones are the dummies?"

Hazel cringed and passed the phone to Mark, who shrugged.

"You think Bob Corker's behind this?" she asked.

"Bring him in for questioning," Ferguson snapped, jabbing his finger at the figures on the floor. "If he's behind this, arrest him. We're all over social media. People think we're a bunch of idiots."

"We'll have them out of the office by the end of the day, Sir," Mark said. "Maybe we could put one in uniform and set it up in the patrol car out on the highway. It might deter speeding."

"Or you could put yourself in the patrol car and catch a few speeders." Ferguson turned on his heel, headed into his glassed-in office and slammed the door.

Hazel shook her head. "I'm not sure how you get away with it, Connors."

"I don't," Mark said, "but someone's gotta lighten things up around here. Ferguson doesn't have a funny bone in his body."

By the end of the day, three more mannequins had been discovered and documented: one found sunbathing in the buff at Stoney Beach, the second reported swimming the backstroke at Orca Point. The third, left anonymously by the detachment's front door was wearing a tuque and plaid shirt with a note pinned to it saying he was found unconscious by the town's fuel dock, an empty beer can beside him. The town was having a field day.

Hazel tried to track Corky down, but he'd left town in the water taxi he operated, taking locals to communities without a road link.

"We have a bloody invasion on our hands," Mark said. "I told Ferguson we'd get these mannequins out of the office by the end of the day. Can you help me move them into the bike lock-up?"

Hazel nodded. "What are the chances of all these mannequins falling off a sailboat or yacht?" she asked as they each dragged a couple toward the side door.

"I'd say zero."

"Maybe they were being shipped somewhere?"

"Duke Point in Nanaimo handles international shipping," Mark said. "I hear they get over fifty thousand containers a year. Maybe one fell overboard and the mannequins managed to make their way north?"

"Gimme a break, Connors." Hazel moved a couple of bikes around in the lock-up while Mark wrestled the stiff bodies toward the far corner. The arms reached out in all directions.

Hazel removed the tuque from the last mannequin to arrive. The head had been damaged. She peered inside. "I wonder what we've got here?"

"Probably not brain matter," Mark guessed as he finished corralling the other mannequins. "Especially since we're dealing with a dummy."

Hazel shook her head and pulled on a pair of latex gloves. After taking photos, she carefully peeled back more of the damaged plastic and removed a small brick-shaped packet wrapped tightly in plastic. "I'm thinking drugs?"

"Maybe." Mark surveyed the other mannequins.

"It could be heroin or meth — maybe even fentanyl," Hazel

said. "We should process this and call in someone who handles drugs."

When they re-entered the office, Ferguson had gone for the day. Hazel called him at home but got no answer. After leaving a message explaining the situation, she called the Criminal Intelligence Unit down-island and spoke with their crime analyst.

"Interesting," Corporal Ryan Woodward said after she brought him up to speed. "I can bring a drug specialist to check things out, but I won't be able to get there till tomorrow. Just keep the package sealed till then. The contents could be toxic."

Hazel agreed, thanked him and disconnected. She passed on the news.

"Shit," Mark said. "People are already calling us dummies. If we bring in some 'expert' to tell us what's in that package, the whole town's gonna think we're morons or lazy."

"If it was a bomb, you'd call the bomb squad," Hazel argued. "If it's fentanyl we need a drug team."

"Good point," said Mark, though she could see he was reluctant. Mark had grown up in Turnaround Bay and knew the town better than the back of his hand. He'd been posted here five years ago, more than happy to come back home after time away. After four months in the small isolated community Hazel still felt like a misfit, but Mark had shown her the ropes, introduced her to locals and kept her from making a fool of herself. He had a sense of humour, but took exception to people who thought they knew more than he did. People with big city egos.

"All of these mannequins could be filled with drugs," Hazel said, "but someone's going to have to cut them open before we find out." They put the package and mannequins in lock-up and called it a day.

Ryan Woodward, the crime analyst and Nina Scott, his drug analyst, arrived the next morning shortly after Hazel and Mark had filled Ferguson in. Following introductions and some handshaking, they set up the interview room with their evidence and left Nina to her investigation.

Back in the office, Hazel thanked Woodward for coming and showed him their file. Woodward, maybe in his mid-thirties, was tall and slim with curly brown hair and blue eyes that reminded her of Liam, her fiancé.

Mark filled the coffee maker while Ferguson paced the office floor, muttering under his breath. Hazel sipped tea from her thermos and chatted with Woodward to the sound of a buzz saw from the interview room.

"I'm curious why someone would go to the trouble of using mannequins to transport drugs," she said. "It sounds like smuggling — but where were the mannequins coming from and where were they headed? We thought they might've fallen off a container ship headed to Nanaimo, but that doesn't explain the drugs . . . or them washing up in Turnaround Bay."

"There were gale force winds in the strait a couple of nights ago," Mark said, joining the conversation. "Someone could've been transporting them by boat and they washed overboard."

Woodward shrugged. "Hiding drugs in mannequins — that's a new one on me. You could be right, though. Let's see what we find."

Nina, the drug analyst, eventually opened the interview room door and let them in. "You're not going to believe what I found," she said.

"Not drugs then?" Hazel guessed.

"Don't keep us in suspense," said Woodward.

"Diamonds."

"Diamonds?" The word echoed through the room.

"Rough, uncut diamonds," Nina said. "There was a packet in

each of the mannequins."

"Mark frowned. "None of this makes sense."

Woodward picked up a plastic evidence bag with some irregularly-shaped clear stones inside. "They could be blood diamonds," he said. "I've heard they're smuggled into the country to hide their illicit origin. They're cut and made into jewellery that's sold as 'mined in Canada.' By the time they're put on the market, their connection to abuse and corruption by warlords in Africa isn't obvious. Someone was planning to make a fortune."

"So how do we track their source?" Hazel asked as she surveyed the room where Nina had decapitated each mannequin in her search for drugs. "If the diamonds were brought into the port in Nanaimo illegally, we need to find out who brought them in and figure out where they were taking them."

"I can assign a couple of members of my team in Nanaimo to find out," Woodward offered. "At this point, we can't directly link the diamonds back to their source . . . but we need to process them as possible evidence of smuggling."

"Then we'll leave you to it," Ferguson jumped in, motioning Mark and Hazel out from the interview room. "It'll let my officers get back to their jobs."

"It looks like the 'experts' are taking over," Mark said as he slumped into the chair at his desk. "That leaves us handing out parking tickets."

Hazel picked up their files on the discovery of each mannequin to photocopy for Woodward. "You're not planning to let that happen, are you?"

Mark shrugged. "Woodward might ask for some local intelligence."

"Am I included in that description?" Hazel asked, smiling.

"Depends where your loyalties lie."

Mark didn't look like he was joking. "What's that supposed to mean?"

"Nobody applies for a posting in Turnaround Bay," he said. "We're a small, remote detachment. We get rookies assigned here right out of training. They bide their time, then leave a trail of dust behind them as soon as they get the chance to transfer out."

"Hey, I asked to come here," said Hazel. "I'm not biding my time." Or was she? Liam was still in Penticton, waiting for her to make up her mind on their future. She glanced down at her left hand where the diamond engagement ring still sparkled on her finger. Where did her commitment lie? Had she made a mistake in coming to Turnaround Bay?

"That's good to know," Mark said, though he didn't look convinced.

Hazel got back to work. She talked with a teenager accused of shoplifting at Peoples Drug Mart and dealt with a break and enter in a vehicle left in the parking lot of Country Grocer's. When she arrived back at the detachment, Mark was sitting at his desk working on a criminal record check for a soccer coach.

"The joys of community policing," he said. "I can count on my fingers the number of high-speed chases I've been involved in." He held up his hands and wiggled his fingers. "I'd even have a few left over."

"Isn't that what you signed up for?"

"Yeah, I know. But I'd give an arm and a leg to be part of catching a gang of diamond smugglers."

"Fingers, arms, legs. What is it about body parts?" Hazel sighed. "Maybe we can get a leg up on the experts. Do some research of our own."

Mark gave a thumbs up just as Nina transferred the evidence bags with the diamonds into the CIU vehicle for identification at a lab in Nanaimo. She signed the chain of custody form and drove away.

The next morning, Hazel woke early enough for a run along her favourite trail. The path meandered under a green canopy of fir, spruce and Western red cedar. The smell from the spruce needles, the sound of waves from the nearby shore and the screaming of seagulls helped wake her senses. After a restless night thinking about blood diamonds and her own diamond, she filled her lungs with salt air, stretched her stride and occasionally reined in Toby, her border collie. After half an hour, she turned around, retraced her steps to her townhouse for a quick shower and breakfast.

Ryan Woodward arrived back at the detachment mid-morning. Ferguson stopped reading the newspaper and asked him into his office.

"It looks like the Criminal Intelligence Unit's in charge," Mark whispered as Hazel tidied her desk. "Think Woodward will appreciate our input?"

Before she could answer, Woodward came out from the office with Ferguson, asked to use their whiteboard and suggested they go over the case together.

"We know six mannequins came ashore in Turnaround Bay," he said. "They ended up on local beaches. That suggests they went overboard from a boat at some point. Mark remembers a storm blowing through a few nights ago," he added. He set out a timeline on the whiteboard. "The mannequins could've been lost then. We don't know where they came from or where they were headed, but I have a couple of guys talking with the port authority in Nanaimo as we speak."

"I searched the internet," Hazel said, taking out her notebook. "There's a company in Victoria that sells mannequins:

Mitchell's Store Fixtures. They might be able to tell us something about their source."

"Good idea." Woodward added the company name to the whiteboard. "Can I leave that with you?"

Hazel nodded and glanced at Mark.

"Has the evidence been confirmed as diamonds?" he asked.

Woodward tapped his felt marker on the palm of his hand. "Yeah. A jeweler had a look. They're diamonds all right. Like I said yesterday, we're a major producer of diamonds, so illegal traders use Canada for laundering their conflict diamonds."

"Like laundering drug money?"

"Exactly," said Woodward. "Blood diamonds are often smuggled through airports, inside baggage — or even body cavities. Using mannequins and bringing them into a port like Nanaimo seems quite a departure."

"We won't be able to track the diamonds to their source, but maybe we can take someone local out of commission," Hazel said. She was appalled by what she'd read about blood diamonds on the RCMP database and the internet last night. Warlords in places like Sierra Leone, Angola and Liberia purchased raw uncut diamonds mined by starving locals under dangerous conditions. They paid a pittance, smuggled the diamonds out of the country, then sold them at a profit. Their source obscured by illegal traders along the supply chain, the conflict diamonds became part of the eighty-billion-dollar global diamond industry, leaving rebels with the cash they needed to finance their violent campaigns to overthrow legitimate governments.

"I'm going to look through our criminal database, see if I can come up with some known crooks on the Island who might have a hand in smuggling." Woodward said, checking his watch. "If I can use your interview room as an office again, I'd appreciate it."

"I can call the Coast Guard and Search and Rescue," Mark offered. "If those mannequins went overboard out in the strait, the vessel could've been in trouble . . . especially during that storm. The Coast Guard would know."

"Good," said Woodward. "That covers a lot of ground."

"Nicely done," Hazel said as Mark sat back down at his desk. "It looks like we're both on the case — unless Ferguson assigns us some paperwork."

Hazel phoned Mitchell's Store Fixtures in Victoria and told the owner about the six mannequins that had come ashore in Turnaround Bay. "We're trying to find out where they're from."

"We import our mannequins from a company in China," John Mitchell said. "They're shipped to Nanaimo, then trucked to us. We haven't ordered any lately so they're not ours."

"What about your customers?" Hazel asked. "Could one of them have imported some mannequins? If you could forward us a list of their names, I can contact them."

"I'm not sure they'd be happy with me turning over their personal information to the police," Mitchell said.

"We're talking about a major criminal case," Hazel persisted, not giving any details. She could understand Mitchell's reluctance to breach his customers' confidentiality but rape, torture, mutilation and slavery were all connected to the illicit diamond trade. "Are you sure you can't pass along a list of names? I know your customers would be willing to cooperate if I explained the situation."

"Come to me with a specific name," Mitchell said. "Then I can tell you if it's someone I've dealt with. Otherwise, I'm sorry, but no."

"I could get a court order," Hazel said.

"You do that," Mitchell said. "I'll talk to you then."

Progress wasn't going to come easy.

The rest of the morning, Hazel sat in the detachment's unmarked SUV beside the Island Highway, holding a radar gun while watching traffic drive by. Policing in Turnaround Bay gave her more variety than her job in Penticton, where she'd spent considerable time in traffic control. At the collision involving Liam, her fiancé, she'd been the first officer on the scene. She'd been overwhelmed by her friend's death and Liam's injuries and hadn't administered a breathalyzer test, never dreaming Liam would drink and drive. But he had. The screw-up was on her record. Another reason for leaving Penticton to start over in Turnaround Bay.

Mark was eating lunch by the time she stepped back into the office after issuing six speeding tickets. "Woodward and Ferguson are out to lunch."

Hazel peered into the large Tupperware container on his desk. "That smells good."

"Ashley's famous spareribs. Leftovers from last night."

"Wish I had someone who cooked for me." She sighed. Most evenings she sat alone at her dinner table eating take-out while she stared at the wall. It would take time to make connections in Turnaround Bay, but she hadn't progressed beyond saying hello and discussing the weather with a few of her neighbours. Being on call 24/7 and wearing a police uniform put a crimp in making friends. She spent what free time she had either running, riding her bike or doing lengths in the pool of a local hotel as part of her triathlon training.

"If you're interested, I'll ask Ashley to cook up one of her specialties and we'll have you over for dinner. I thought maybe you were too busy to spend time with us locals."

"Dinner sounds great . . . and I'm available any time."

"I wonder how the Criminal Intelligence Unit's doing?" Mark said, changing the subject. "I can't figure out why it would take two of their 'experts' to deal with the Nanaimo Port Authority. I could call them from here to see if they're missing a shipment of dummies."

"What about the Coast Guard and Search and Rescue? Any luck there?"

Mark licked his fingers. "The Coast Guard's installed some new radar stations to provide better information on vessel movement in the strait, but they haven't noticed anything suspicious in the past few days. No reports of collisions, no capsized boats, no drownings. Search and Rescue got a distress call during that storm a few nights ago, but it was a fishing boat on its way to Port Hardy. The skipper had trouble with his engine and was hours overdue. They found his boat dead in the water and had to tow it."

Hazel started into the sandwich she'd picked up at the deli.

Mark scowled. "What *is* that you're eating?"

"An eggplant, tomato and spinach sandwich."

"You sure you don't want some of these spareribs?"

"No, but thanks. I have paperwork to fill out on these speeders."

Hazel was ready to head home for a long bike ride when Ryan Woodward came out from the interview room with an update on his team's progress.

"According to the warehouse manager at Duke Point, a shipment of a dozen mannequins arrived a week ago from China. Guess who the bill of lading was made out to?"

"China?" Hazel said. "That fellow from Mitchell Store Fixtures in Victoria who brings in mannequins from China?"

"One and the same."

"He was pretty tight lipped," she said. "And he told me he didn't have any mannequins on order."

"Well, I suspect he was lying," said Woodward. "All the paperwork was made out to his company. Twelve mannequins were picked up from the port the day of that storm by a trucking company."

"Then why did the mannequins end up in Turnaround Bay instead of Victoria?"

"We're still digging into that."

"I got in touch with the Coast Guard and Search and Rescue," Mark said. "They have nothing suspicious to report from out in the strait. Without a description of the boat we're looking for there's nothing to go on."

Woodward shrugged. "We're still looking for the other six mannequins that arrived in Nanaimo. They were all headed up-island for some reason. Whoever's involved doesn't know we're on to them so they might still be in this area. Not many people have the skill to cut raw diamonds into gem-quality jewels. If they've hired someone local, that might explain why the mannequins came here."

Hazel sighed. "So, we're looking for a local diamond-cutter and an anonymous boat?"

"My guys have gone to Victoria to question John Mitchell," Woodward said. "Without any other leads, I'm calling it a day."

"I could get a list of marinas between here and Nanaimo," Mark said. "Make some calls to see if anyone's spotted a boat with a dozen dummies onboard. You'd think they'd remember."

"Good idea. If we knew what boat we were looking for we could send out a search." Woodward smiled and picked up his jacket. "Can I buy either of you dinner before I go back to my motel?"

Mark lifted the lid of his laptop. "Don't tempt me with food when I'm on a mission."

"I have a dog waiting for me at home," Hazel said, "but thanks for the offer." Woodward was charming, but the last thing she needed at the moment was another man in her life.

The dark clouds overhead were dumping buckets of rain the next morning as Hazel sprinted from her jeep to the detachment's side door. Locals grew webbed feet, apparently, so unless something changed, she was still an outsider.

Inside, Mark was already calling marinas. He gave a thumbs up. "We're gonna find that damned boat, come hell or high water."

"Which comes first?" She shook out her raincoat and set down a container of yogurt and thermos of tea.

"Some phone calls." He handed her a list of marinas to call.

She sat down at her desk and picked up the office phone. "There's nothing sexy about this kind of police work," she said. "People have no idea what we spend our time doing."

Mark snorted. "Hey, we're tracking down smugglers. Don't knock it. I can just see the headlines: Turnaround Bay RCMP capture smugglers, intercepting diamonds worth billions. My name would appear right after the headline."

"Dream on."

Half an hour later, Hazel was speaking with a marina owner in Telegraph Cove who mentioned a boat that had docked with fuel problems.

"I got suspicious when the skipper didn't let me come aboard to check his fuel line."

"Maybe he was hiding something?"

"My thoughts exactly," the marina owner said. "There were two people onboard when it docked. I had a funny feeling about it so I recorded the boat's registration number and the name on the hull. *A Girl's Best Friend.*"

Hazel wrote down the number and a description of the boat in her notebook. "It sounds like just the boat I'm looking for," she said. "Any idea where it was going?"

"Sorry, all I can say is it's headed your way. The boat's

captain wasn't talking much. I have them on video if that's any help."

Hazel asked him to hang on to the video and thanked him. When she reported what she'd discovered, Mark pumped his fist in the air. "Think we should pass on our intel to Woodward or track down the boat on our own?"

"Come on, Mark, we're all in this together. We want the same thing."

"Fame and fortune?"

"No. Law and order."

"There's just the small matter about who gets the credit," Mark said. "The Criminal Intelligence Unit or us?"

"Why does it matter?" Hazel sensed that it did matter to Mark. He'd spent the past four years as a cop in Turnaround Bay, getting little credit and lots of flack for keeping the peace.

The decision was taken out of their hands when Ryan Woodward came into the office. "What's up?" he asked.

Hazel updated him on her suspicion about *A Girl's Best Friend*.

"Well done." Woodward helped himself to a stale cup of coffee from the coffeemaker. "The officers I sent to Victoria questioned John Mitchell. He still insists he didn't order any mannequins, so we took a second look at the bill of lading. It seems someone knew about Mitchell's occasional orders for mannequins from China and decided to use his business name to transport some diamonds. When the mannequins arrived in Nanaimo, the port called the phone number on the bill of lading. The number wasn't Mitchell's, though. It was bogus. A white panel van showed up with enough paperwork to collect the cargo from Customs. Surveillance video coverage at the warehouse got us the van's license number and a description of the two men who loaded them into the vehicle. Unfortunately, the van was reported stolen earlier that day, then ditched shortly after the mannequins were picked up."

"Too bad," Hazel said. "They weren't taking any chances about being tracked. Anything we can do from here?"

"Thanks to you, we now have a boat name with a registration number to trace. Maybe just keep your eyes open. I'm going to spend some time on the water, see if I can find *A Girl's Best Friend*."

Hazel wished him luck just as Sergeant Ferguson marched out from his office.

"What are you two up to?" he grumbled. "At least one of you should be out on patrol. People need to see we're keeping them safe."

While Mark got ready to pound the pavement, he showed Hazel the pedometer his wife, Ashley, had given him as a birthday gift.

"I'd have to walk ten miles just to wear off lunch," he complained. "I'm not sure this thing's gonna be any help." He clipped the monitor to his utility belt. "Ashley thinks I should lose some weight, then she tempts me with her home cooking. It's a losing battle."

"Let's see how many miles you can put in," said Hazel.

A phone call from a woman about a stolen bicycle interrupted her. She scribbled down the address.

"Want to go for a car ride instead?" she asked Mark, eyeing Ferguson who was sitting in his office as usual.

"Definitely beats walking," he said and pulled on his vest.

They got into the patrol car with Mark in the driver's seat. "What kind of bike is it?" he asked.

"The woman didn't say. As far as I know it's got two wheels." Hazel's triathlon bike had high end components. It was expensive — over six thousand dollars. When she wasn't riding, she parked it in her spare bedroom for safekeeping.

Seal Cove Road was home to a number of small industries, a couple of lodges and some rural acreages. Mark drove past them, then through several kilometres of undeveloped forest before they came to a small subdivision of houses built round a cul-de-sac.

Mark whistled. "A bike with a motor would be handy out here. We're fifteen kilometres from town."

"I do seventy before breakfast every Sunday."

Mark cringed. "I'm trying not to think about what that would do to my butt."

They stopped at a driveway and Hazel checked the address. The brand-new shake and shingle house had a waterfront view. Alder trees turning fall colours edged the yard and the newly laid lawn was still green and weedless.

The woman who answered Mark's knock was tall and slim, maybe in her forties, with short hair spiked with gel. She was wearing black spandex tights and a sweatshirt that matched her pink lipstick.

"I understand you're missing a bicycle," Mark said, after introductions.

Merilee Tsolakis explained that she'd heard a commotion outside in the carport during the night but hadn't thought much of it until she was ready to go for a ride and realized her bike was missing.

Hazel tried to sound sympathetic as she took down particulars, but bikes that weren't locked up or tied down were an easy target for thieves. "It sounds expensive," she said when Merilee mentioned the brand. "Have you checked with any of your neighbours? They might've seen or heard something suspicious."

"No. We just moved in. I don't know the neighbours yet." She pointed to a house with three vehicles parked in the driveway. "Those ones are noisy."

Hazel reassured Merilee they'd try to locate her bike. On the way back to the patrol car, Mark suggested they question the neighbours.

"This subdivision's new; I don't know who lives out here yet," he said. "It'll give us a chance to peek inside some houses — see what people are up to."

"Sure. Nothing wrong with gaining local intelligence."

As they approached the house with the noisy neighbours, Hazel scanned the site. The house, a two-storey, flat-roofed building with yellow siding, had only one small window on the second floor. A two-car garage with white vinyl doors gave no indication of what lay inside. Someone obviously enjoyed their privacy.

Before ringing the doorbell, Hazel peered round the side of the house and noticed an empty boat trailer. There was no sign of a boat or Merilee's bike. She could hear raised angry voices inside.

When Mark knocked on the door, the voices went quiet. A young man in his twenties answered.

"Good afternoon," Hazel said, trying to get a look past the man who was blocking the entry. She introduced herself and Mark then explained that the man's neighbour, Ms. Tsolakis, was missing a bike. "It was taken sometime last night."

The man crossed his arms, shrugged and checked his watch. So much for being neighbourly.

"Did you notice any suspicious vehicles yesterday or hear someone out on the street last night?" Mark asked.

"I don't live here," the man said. "My uncle does."

"And your uncle's name would be?" Hazel readied her pen and notebook.

"John." The man glanced over his shoulder.

"And his last name?" Hazel went on. She suspected the occupants of the house knew there were cops at the door.

"What does this matter? My uncle's retired. He moved here to get away from nosy neighbours."

"And you are?"

"Jim."

Hazel wondered why Jim, if that was really his name, was bothered by their questions. Something didn't seem quite right. "Can I speak with your uncle?" she asked, still smiling.

"He's out at the moment. I'll ask him about the bicycle when he gets home." Jim's grey eyes kept shifting toward their patrol car and he started kicking at the doorjamb. He was about to close the door on them when Mark took over.

"This is quite the location," he said. "How long has your uncle lived here?"

Jim shrugged.

"Mind if I take a peek at the view he gets of the water?" Mark went on.

Before Jim could answer, Mark strolled around the corner of the house. Jim bolted after him, leaving Hazel alone at the entry. Curious, she nudged the door open, peeked inside and came face to face with a mannequin. She let out a small squeak and covered her mouth. Shit. Several decapitated mannequins stood upright in a closet to the right of the door in what looked like a mudroom. Her heart pounded wildly as she used her cell phone to snap a few photos. She stepped back from the doorway just as Mark sauntered around the corner, Jim in his wake.

Hazel gulped down the lump in her throat. They'd found the smugglers — holed up in Turnaround Bay. Trying not to tip off Jim that she was on to him, she thanked him for his help and shook hands. "If you or your uncle John notice anyone suspicious, just give us a call." She led Mark back to the patrol car, forcing herself to slow down as she got in. At the intersection to the main road, she asked him to stop.

"It's the bloody diamond smugglers," she blurted.

"What?"

"While you went sightseeing, I poked my nose into the house

and saw half a dozen mannequins." She shook her head. "These are the guys we're looking for."

Mark tapped his head then gave a thumbs up. "Local intelligence. I knew it would come in handy. My bullshit detector went off while we were talking to Jim so I thought I'd have a look around. I got a good view of the living room from the other side of the house," he said. "There were five men sitting round a table. It didn't look like they were playing Monopoly."

Hazel picked up the radio to contact the detachment. When Mira answered, she asked if Ferguson was available. "I believe he's still out to lunch," she said.

"Can you track him down, tell him to call me ASAP." Hazel disconnected and picked up her own phone to call Ryan Woodward.

"Constable Quinn, good news," he said when he answered. "I'm with four officers from the Marine Services Unit. They were patrolling in this area so I joined up with them. We've located *A Girl's Best Friend*. It's at a private marina just south of Turnaround Bay. Nobody's onboard at the moment, so we have it under surveillance."

Hazel congratulated him, then filled him in on their situation. "We counted at least six men in the house," she said. "I'm afraid we might've tipped them off with our questions. They could be getting ready to split. If we want to catch them red-handed, we need to act fast." She gave Woodward the address of the house and its location.

"We're on our way," Woodward said. "Just wait till we get there."

Hazel disconnected. She checked her rear-view mirror just as a car came into view from around the corner. If it was the smugglers they were in trouble.

Luckily, it was Merilee Tsolakis who stopped and rolled down her window. "Is everything okay?" she asked, looking puzzled.

Mark nodded. "Just dandy, ma'am. We haven't found your bike yet, but we're on the lookout. You have a nice day now."

Within half an hour, two unmarked SUVs pulled up beside the Turnaround Bay patrol car. Ryan Woodward jumped out.

"You two okay?"

"Great," Mark said. He smiled as he stepped out from their vehicle.

"We did a property title search on the way here," Woodward said. "The house is owned by an Ivan Petrovsky. From what we can tell he's a retired diamond-cutter from Antwerp. He's a foreign national . . . only been in the country a few months. We also obtained a telewarrant to search the property."

Hazel was impressed. "Nice work."

"You can thank my team in Nanaimo."

"I saw six mannequins in the house," Hazel said. "I expect they're cutting the diamonds that were stashed inside them."

"Then let's catch the bastards," Mark said and rubbed his hands together.

"That's the plan. You with us?" Woodward turned to Hazel.

When she nodded and Mark gave a thumbs up, the team pored over a Google map of the cul-de-sac while discussing their entry. Mark filled them in with a description of the house itself, including the doors and windows he'd seen as he circled the house. Woodward divided them into pairs that would fan out to cover the property from all angles. Everyone got into one of the SUVs and Woodward drove toward their target. Hazel felt for her holster, hoping things would go according to plan. Inside the vehicle, the team from the Marine Services Unit spoke in whispers and Mark sat in silence, worry lines creasing his forehead.

Woodward stopped before the house came into view. Hazel jumped out from the vehicle, with Mark just behind her. They quickly made their way into the woods. Staying within tree cover, they moved closer to the property. Once the house was in sight, she crouched and crept forward. She craned her neck to see what was going on, then ducked.

"Someone's on the deck," she whispered to Mark. "I think it's Petrovsky's nephew."

A loud knock on the door was their signal. Hazel sprinted from the woods to the house and tried to blend in with the wall. Mark joined her, gasping for breath. She peered around the corner. Their suspect was doing a runner so she stepped out from cover.

"Police. Hold it right there," she shouted, drawing her gun. The man froze. "Raise your arms," she called while covering the distance between them. Her hand was shaking slightly, the sound of her heart hammering in her ears.

Mark joined her and wrestled the man into handcuffs.

"Nicely done," she said.

A male voice from inside the house yelled, "All clear. We have the house under control."

Hazel and Mark helped take the house occupants into custody. It took hours of work before they were hauled off to Nanaimo. The evidence from the house and video coverage from the Nanaimo Port Authority should be enough to lay charges of smuggling. At this point they were unlikely to track down the original source of the diamonds and make an arrest there, but they'd put the gang who was laundering them out of business.

"It's a good thing your bullshit detector kicked in when we were talking to Petrovsky's nephew," Hazel said. She pulled on a pair of booties and latex gloves to enter the house with the evidence. "This whole take-down wouldn't have happened without you."

"If you hadn't been curious and poked your nose inside, these guys would still be cutting diamonds."

"Local intelligence." Hazel said.

"You got it." He gave her a high five.

The headless mannequins stood eerily near the entry as Hazel walked past them. The expensively furnished house had a breathtaking view of the strait from the living room.

Mark stopped next to a large coffee table. "Check out those diamonds."

Hazel shrugged. Diamonds had lost their appeal. They were supposed to be the way to a girl's heart... a girl's best friend. In reality they were the product of an industry that manipulated availability and inflated their product's market value.

She glanced at her hand. She'd taken off her engagement ring this morning. She would send it back to Liam. Tell him their engagement was finished. She couldn't continue a relationship with someone she didn't trust. She'd start over here in Turnaround Bay.

"Look at this...," Mark said, interrupting her thoughts. He was pointing to a diamond necklace displayed on a black velvet bust on the kitchen island. "Ashley would love it."

"Don't even think about it," Hazel said. "I bet a night out in a restaurant with candles and a bouquet of flowers would impress her."

"You sure?"

"Positive."

"Oh, yeah. Ashley wants you to come to dinner some day this week," Mark said. "She said if you like barbecued salmon, I get to cook it."

"Lucky you, it's my favourite," Hazel said. "How about Friday?"

3

SALTY DOG BLUES
BY WINONA KENT

It was 2012, and I was working as an entertainer on board the *Star Sapphire*, a former ocean liner that had been repurposed by StarSea Cruises for the summer run between Vancouver and Alaska. Jason Davey, TopDeck Lounge, performing all your vocal and instrumental favourites, Eight 'til Late. My real last name's Figgis, but I have well-known musical parents, and back then — as now — I wanted to distance myself from their fame.

For lifesaving and accommodation purposes I was considered crew. But for all social activities, including food and drink, I was the equivalent of an officer. I enjoyed the freedom of the ship, upstairs and down.

All our guests had boarded, we'd done our mandatory passenger muster, and we were on our way to Juneau. I had about an hour before I was due onstage, so I went downstairs for an early supper.

"Detached retinas," said Barrie, our chief purser, as I sat down with my selection from the self-service buffet. Every evening in the officers' mess the chefs picked the least popular item from the passenger menu and let us have it for dinner. That night it was spaghetti Bolognese. "That's a new one."

"Medical emergency?" I inquired.

"Miss Abigail Ferryman." Quentin, our assistant purser, a fine young lad from Scotland, hated spaghetti and had opted for a large plate of Caesar salad with triple helpings of grated parmesan. "She claims to have an allergy to the colour blue. She informed us it would cause her retinas to detach. Amongst other things. I've arranged to have all offending items removed from her cabin. Though the carpeting may prove to be a bit of a stumbling block."

"She's travelling with a service dog," Barrie added.

"For her allergy?" I also hated spaghetti, but I had a three-hour gig ahead of me and I needed the carbs. I bribed myself by dousing it with some generous dollops of hot sauce.

"The wee doggie's name is Lord Fothergill," Quentin replied. "Though I've decided to call him Spike. If no one objects."

"Spike might," I said.

"'Wee' being the operative word this afternoon, just after Sailaway," Barrie said. "Against a chair leg. In the Atrium Room."

"Offended by the décor?" I guessed. The principal colours in the Atrium Room were shades of green. No possibility of detached retinas.

"Bloody service dogs," Barrie muttered.

"I thought we provided special places for service dogs to . . . wee," I said.

"Oh, we do, Jason. But Lord Fothergill apparently has an easily irritated and very impatient bladder."

"That'll be strike one then," Quentin said humorously. "Failure to use the designated relief area. And with all due respect, Spike is not a true service dog. He merely provides emotional support."

"I'll be needing emotional support by the time we dock in Juneau," Barrie said.

I went back to my cabin to change into my gigging togs. On the way, I walked past Seawind, the passenger dining room, to see if I could spot Spike and his owner.

It wasn't difficult. Miss Ferryman was a large woman with flowing red hair, wearing a royal purple kaftan with gold embroidery. Spike, a Chihuahua, was sporting a matching shirt and leggings, as well as a glittering gold collar embellished with a purple feather that looked like something he'd stolen from a stripper. Spike and his owner had availed themselves of a table near the door and Spike, standing on his hind legs on a chair, was happily chowing down on hamburger from our Sailaway dinner menu.

"'Evening," I said to Marcello, our *maître d'*, who was giving Spike the evil eye.

"It is not a good evening at all," Marcello replied. "Chef Franco is livid. That . . . animal . . . has defiled his most favourite Sailaway creation."

"Really . . . ?" Chef Franco had only been on board for three weeks, but already had a reputation for his inordinately fierce temper. Our Seawind burger seemed hardly worth getting upset over.

"Seafood turnover with lobster sauce," the *maître d'* corrected. "He wolfed it down . . . and then . . . ."

Marcello leaned towards me confidentially.

"He . . . vomited!"

"Oh dear," I said. "Defiled indeed."

"His owner demanded more food. And so, what you see."

I *tsk'd* my sympathetic disapproval.

"And that . . . animal . . . should be on the floor."

"Check the chair legs after they leave," I suggested. "And ask Housekeeping for stain and odour remover. Just a thought."

As I exited, I could hear Spike snorting his opinion of Chef

Franco's lobster sauce. As I opened the Crew Only door in the Seawind foyer, I heard something that sounded suspiciously like a water glass smashing. And as I walked down the stairs to my cabin, I could hear Chef Franco's outraged baritone voice exclaiming something not very polite in broken English, punctuated with furious Italian.

Downstairs, it was noisy and claustrophobic, only a deck away from the Engine Room. One main thoroughfare with side passageways leading off to crew cabins, stores and utilities, the ship's laundry. Glaring fluorescents, overhead pipes, lino floors. The constant roar of the turbines. No portholes — we were down at the waterline. Watertight doors, ten of them, bow to stern. I was lucky — I had a cabin to myself. Others had to share.

I changed into a bright blue silk shirt, sleeves rolled fashionably up between wrist and elbow, and black trousers and went back upstairs to play.

You don't see ships like the *Sapphire* anymore. SOLAS, the international treaty for Safety Of Life At Sea that sets safety standards for ships, has done away with vessels that don't meet minimum safety requirements, and passengers demand more activities and entertainment than we could ever have provided. She may have been old and creaky, but our little *Sapphire* had six times more character than those bang-for-buck floating resorts with eighteen passenger decks, nineteen restaurants, twenty pools, four water slides, a go-kart track and a golf course bolted on top of a barge.

As I waited for the passenger lift outside the dining room, I spotted a man and a woman in matching turquoise windbreakers trying to make sense out of the deck plan bolted to the wall.

"Can I help?" I inquired. "You Are Here." I pointed out

where we were. There had once been a red dot stuck to the diagram, but it had been worn away.

"We're trying to find our cabin," said the man.

"He forgot the map," said his wife. "He left it on the bed."

"What deck is your cabin on?" I asked.

"The one where the shops are," the woman replied.

The ship had eleven decks in total, though the bottom three were reserved for crew and the engine room. The officers' mess and the Seawind Dining Room were on Deck 4 — Caribe.

Deck 5 — Baja — had passenger cabins and the Showcase Lounge, home of our nightly cabaret. Deck 6 — Aloha — had more cabins and the purser's desk.

Deck 7 — Promenade — was where our passengers boarded and where the Atrium Room was, as well as the shopping arcade, which was located just outside the Atrium Room's entrance doors. And towards the Prom's bow were the "expensive" cabins — the ship's old first class staterooms from her transatlantic days.

"There you are," I said, tapping the map. "Forward Prom. Up at the posh end."

"Thank you!" said the man. "Do you work on board?"

I showed him my name tag, which was in my trousers pocket and which I should have been wearing. But it gets in the way of my guitar, so I never put it on when I'm playing.

"TopDeck Lounge," I said. "I'm the featured entertainment."

"Do you do requests?" the woman asked, clearly impressed.

"Of course."

"Then we'll see you there!"

I rode in the lift with them as far as Prom and then continued on my own to Deck 8 — Lido — which had outside decks, an informal cafe and the casino and then Deck 9 — sports — which was the home of the ship's library and, next to it, the TopDeck Lounge, where I was installed for your nightly listening pleasure.

We were directly underneath the bridge, which was on Deck

10 — Sun — and Deck 11 — Observation — where you could always find the best views of the passing coastal wilderness and, if you were lucky, a whale or two.

It was dark and we were zigzagging through Seymour Narrows — a passage Captain George Vancouver once called one of the vilest stretches of water in the world. That was when Ripple Rock still existed — an immense and inconvenient hazard which was removed in a planned explosion in 1958. But the tide in the Narrows can still top sixteen knots, which is why Alaska-bound cruise ships always try to beat it by leaving Vancouver a good few hours before sunset.

My job was to play my guitar and sing. I had assorted other trickery, including backing tracks, to enhance my performance and impress the guests.

It was past ten o'clock and most of the first sitting post-meal passengers had drifted off to bed, replaced by second sitting, who tended to be younger, more energetic and less reliant on medications. I glanced over the audience as I worked through my usual assortment of Sailaway tunes.

There was Danny, the ship's photographer, off-duty and enjoying a drink with Diandra, one of the shoppies, still in her uniform — a white shirt with a distinctive little black and white silk scarf, and a black skirt, short and pencil-tight. Danny and Diandra had been an item for the past couple of months.

There was an anemic-looking guy who was undergoing psychiatric counselling to help him get over his pathological fear of dogs (he'd said so in a very loud voice to Carla, that week's waitress, as she took his order).

And sitting at the table beside him, the couple wearing the matching turquoise windbreakers — who'd spent my entire set texting on their cellphones.

And then I spotted *them* walking into the room: Miss Ferryman with her royal purple kaftan and flowing red hair, and Spike with his feather, looking for trouble.

The anemic-looking guy bolted out of the lounge without finishing his drink as Carla placed a little glass dish of mixed bar snacks on Miss Ferryman's table.

"Bring us something else," Miss Ferryman demanded. "Lord Fothergill dislikes peanuts."

"I'm afraid we don't have anything else," Carla replied. And then: "Does he have an allergy?"

"Are you making fun of me? Lord Fothergill enjoys perfect health. Take this abomination away, remove the peanuts and bring it back."

Carla valued her job. "What can I get you to drink?" she inquired, placing the little dish on her tray.

"A Parfait d'Amour for me and an Evian water for Lord Fothergill. Served at room temperature. In a china bowl."

"Would you mind putting your dog on the floor?" Carla asked.

"Lord Fothergill dislikes the floor. He prefers a chair."

"I'm really sorry, but service animals are not allowed to sit on the furniture. Also, he should be on a leash or a harness . . . ."

Miss Ferryman stared at Carla.

"A Parfait d'Amour," she said, "and an Evian water. Room temperature. In a china bowl." Carla walked back to the bar.

I finished my song — "Beyond the Sea" — to a smattering of applause. Carla brought me a chilled melon juice — my favourite nightly tipple. I decided on "Sail On, Sailor," the Beach Boys tune, while Carla returned the nut-less bar snacks to Miss Ferryman's table.

That's when Spike jumped down from his chair and trotted across to my setup in the middle of the dance floor.

"*Go away*," I said, under my breath, between verses.

But Spike was having none of it.

In fact, he decided to sing along. Loudly.

I seriously doubt Brian Wilson ever considered a howling Chihuahua when he co-wrote the lyrics for my vocal offering. I smoothly segued into something else by the Beach Boys that could accommodate a howl in Spike's key — "I Get Around" — and improvised a duet, which made my audience laugh.

Not content to simply join my act, Spike wandered around to the back of the stage to see if he could make it as a roadie.

"Don't even think about it," I said.

But Spike was investigating my amp.

"No!" I said, in no uncertain terms. "Bad dog!"

But it was too late. Spike's leg was up . . . .

There was a thunderous buzz as the fuse inside my amp shorted out . . . followed by limp silence from my guitar.

I'm not sure what "Fuck you, Jason" is in Chihuahua-speak, but it sounds a lot like "*yeyurp*" and there's a derisive snort at the end for added emphasis.

I stood up, retrieved Spike from the floor and carried him at arm's length, like a baby with a whiffy nappy, back to his owner.

"Your dog," I said, plopping him back on his chair.

"Lord Fothergill is impressed with your mastery of the guitar," Miss Ferryman replied. "Please do continue."

If that was admiration, I'd have loved to have seen what Spike did to musicians he hated.

I carried on my set with just my acoustic Gibson and a good deal of singing. By midnight, the lounge was empty and I was serenading Samuel and Carla and Javier, a deck steward who'd sneaked in for three tins of Guinness and a nearly-full bottle of Blue Curacao. Javier was from Argentina and was disembarking for his six-weeks' leave on Monday when we docked in Juneau. He was obviously in a mood for early celebrations.

"That animal," said Barrie, our chief purser, at breakfast as he chowed down on stewed prunes and Special K, "will be the death of me."

"That animal will be the death of my show," I replied.

While I was having my scrambled eggs, sausage and toast, the ship's electricians were examining my amp. I had spare fuses. But Spike's piss must have contained some kind of secret Chihuahua corrosive. The wires, and everything else within three inches of his target, were shot.

Our conversation was interrupted by Quentin, who'd left ten minutes earlier to go to work, but had now rushed back.

"Sorry, sir," he said, to Barrie, "but you're wanted upstairs. It seems late last night the wee doggie was spotted in the aft jacuzzi and some of the guests have complained."

"Fucking hell," Barrie said, pushing back from the table.

"Can I come too?" I inquired.

Not only had Spike been enjoying a post-concert splash in the Promenade Deck hot tub—it seemed he'd also obviously decided it would be an excellent spot to have a bowel movement. His contribution to the décor had been plopped prominently onto the jacuzzi's apron. Putting the poop back in poop deck, as it were.

The lineup at the purser's desk consisted of Javier (the unfortunate deck steward who'd been summoned to remove Spike's droppings), as well as Peter, the head pool butler (who Javier reported to); Chef Franco and Marcello, both intent on lodging their complaints concerning Spike's dining habits; Diandra, the shoppie, who'd been chased around the jewellery counter as she'd closed up for the evening; Belinda, the retail sales manager who looked after the entire shopping arcade and was nicknamed "The Dragon Lady," mostly because of her unsympathetic tirades towards her employees; and Diandra's boyfriend Danny, the photographer, who'd been pissed on as he'd put up all of yesterday's passenger embarkation shots in the picture gallery.

There were also a handful of guests with harrowing tales of unsolicited contact, including the anemic psychiatric patient whose name, it transpired, was Mr. Bothwell; and the texting duo in the matching windbreakers who, it turned out, were called Mitch and Honey.

"I want you to know we'll be discussing this very serious disruption to our perfect holiday on Twitter and Facebook," Honey was saying, jabbing her cellphone into the air to make her point.

"I really wish you wouldn't," Barrie said. "And I hope you'll consider that we're working to resolve the problem to the best of our abilities and with our guests' health and comfort foremost in our efforts. I'll be extending each of you a $100 credit for drinks to show our appreciation for your patience and understanding."

I'd situated myself on the aft Promenade, snaffling one of the wooden imitation steamer chairs and a couple of padded cushions while I checked Twitter on my phone.

It was a glorious Sunday and the passing scenery, as ever, was spectacular. We'd spent the night cruising Johnstone Strait and Discovery Passage. We were just about to adjust our course towards Triple Island where we'd exchange our Canadian pilots for ones from Southeastern Alaska.

I was scanning for disgruntled #starsapphire hashtags when a shadow fell over my little screen. I looked up. It was, of course, Quentin.

"Sorry to bother you, Jason, but Miss Ferryman's having a wee turn and she's asking for you."

"Why me?" I said.

"Apparently Spike's gone missing."

"And she thinks I had something to do with it?"

"Not at all. She's asking for your assistance."

"I don't understand. Why?"

"I believe it may have to do with some reluctance on the part of ship's security to launch an investigation. And the fact that she insists Spike has taken a strong liking to you. Will you come?"

I love a good mystery.

I knocked on Miss Ferryman's door.

"Who's that?"

"Jason Davey."

"Who?"

"The musician," I said, patiently. "You wanted to see me?"

"Yes! Come in."

Miss Ferryman's cabin was one of the former first class staterooms up at the forward end of the Promenade Deck. It now looked anything but. The two large square windows overlooking our long bow were minus their curtains. The marine blue bedspread had been removed, exposing the tan brown blankets that were standard in all our cabins. Sheets had been draped over the two armchairs, and the entire floor was covered in a white tarpaulin that I'd last seen up near the funnel in Skagway, where the painters had been dealing with some rust.

Miss Ferryman had arranged herself on the bed in a pose reminiscent of something from a silent-era film where the dialogue text frame would have contained one word: *Distraught.*

Spike's bed — an upholstered purple indulgence — lay beside her pillow, forlorn and empty.

"Sit," she commanded, waving at a sheet-covered armchair.

I sat.

"I am unwell," she said.

"I'm sorry to hear that." I'd done the StarSea course in customer relations. They told us never to apologize for anything. I made a point of breaking the rule whenever I could.

"Lord Fothergill is missing."

"So I was told. But he can't have gone far."

"He's been abducted."

"Why do you think that?" I asked.

"Lord Fothergill would never deliberately leave my side. He is devoted to me."

"How is it he went missing, then?"

"We were taking our exercise along the Enclosed Promenade. I was momentarily distracted by the ship's photographer who was attempting to take my picture for his ridiculous display board. After I dismissed him, I looked for Lord Fothergill. But he was gone."

"And what time was this?" I asked.

"Immediately after breakfast. Ten o'clock."

To my mind, 10 a.m. wasn't quite 'immediately after breakfast.' But to each his own.

"And you didn't have him on a leash?" I asked.

"Lord Fothergill despises confinement. Leashes create anxiety."

"And what was he wearing when you last saw him?" I inquired, imitating my favourite TV police procedurals in a lame attempt to humour her.

Miss Ferryman failed to be amused. "A red and white hand-knitted cardigan and a matching scarf. It was chilly on deck. And his feather, of course. It was a bequeathment from his grandfather, who received it as a gift from a prominent member of the royal family when he was awarded the Freedom of the Palace and the beloved friendship of Her

Majesty's Corgis. Lord Fothergill always displays it on his collar."

"And you had a good look for him . . . ?"

"Of course I did," Miss Ferryman snapped. "Do you take me for an idiot? I searched fruitlessly for over an hour."

"Is it possible," I said, carefully, "that he might have fallen overboard?"

"It is not," Miss Ferryman replied. "Lord Fothergill is a seasoned traveller. He's accompanied me on numerous cruises. He would not have gone anywhere near the railings."

"And what did you do next?"

"I went to see the chief purser. He referred me to your chief security officer."

Our chief security officer, Kevin Blaney, was sixty-three years old and trained in antiterrorism. He'd once done highly classified things with the British navy. I was sure the thought of investigating a potential dognapping would thrill him to no end.

"Mr. Blaney informed me he would look into it. This isn't good enough. I want an investigation. Now."

"I'm not sure what you think I can do . . . ."

"Lord Fothergill is very fond of you."

"He pissed on my amp," I said.

"As I informed you last night, it was an expression of his affection. He thinks the world of you. I wish you to intercede."

"I'm sure Mr. Blaney is doing his best to track him down."

"I'm sure he isn't," Miss Ferryman snapped.

"When the photographer was trying to take your picture this morning, do you remember if there was anyone else in the general vicinity?"

"Nobody. I was quite alone."

"Are you absolutely certain?"

Miss Ferryman considered me, and then said, "There was a woman from one of the shops. I saw her fleetingly."

"And you're sure she was from the shops?"

"Of course. I recognized her clothing."

"And what was she doing?"

"She was standing in the doorway. Looking out."

"The doorway that leads from the foyer to the Enclosed Promenade?"

"Yes. The very one."

"Was she doing anything else?"

"Not that I could see."

"Would you recognize her again?"

"I suppose I would."

"Could you come with me and point her out?"

It was inconvenient, of course. But Miss Ferryman obviously thought the better of complaining. I was Spike's only hope.

We left her cabin and she marched down to the shopping arcade.

"There," she said, pointing at Diandra who'd been protesting at the purser's desk earlier. "That one. Do you suspect her?"

"I suspect everyone," I said.

"Fuck that dog," Kevin Blaney said in his office on Aloha Deck. His walls were covered with pictures of submarines and fighter jets. He had a photo on his desk of a dozen men in scuba gear and wetsuits, arranged in two rows, their faces deliberately obscured by masks and mouthpieces.

"I thought perhaps he'd fallen overboard, and suggested it to Miss Ferryman, but she was adamant he hadn't."

"He hasn't fallen overboard," Kev confirmed.

"You know that for a fact, do you? Have you checked the CCTVs?"

The *Sapphire* didn't have much by way of high-tech security. There were a couple of cams installed on the Promenade Deck but that was about it.

"Trust me, Jason."

"Can I look at the footage?"

"No."

"Do you know where he is?"

"No."

"It's a small ship. Not a lot of places to hide a yappy Chihuahua. Is he still alive?"

"Stay out of it, Jason. For your own wellbeing. And the dog's."

I was pretty certain Kevin knew what had happened to Lord Fothergill. And was probably protecting whoever had taken him. But I didn't want to end up bundled into a rope locker, my desperate cries for help ignored until we docked in Juneau. Spike was still with us and that's all I needed to know.

They sold everything in the shopping arcade, from fleece jackets embossed with StarSea's logo to 'personal convenience' items, to high end cosmetics and, of course, jewellery and ceramic figurines. I did a circuit of the Tanzanite counter where Diandra had been accosted by Spike the night before.

Diandra was not the jewellery specialist. Her post was on the other side of the foyer, where they sold toothpaste and Aspirin. And that's where I found her, arguing with Danny, who was attempting to buy seasickness tablets. She appeared to be trying to prevent it.

She lost the argument. Danny signed for the tablets and stormed out of the arcade.

"Lover's tiff?" I inquired boldly, presenting her with a tube of Colgate for Sensitive Teeth.

"I told him to visit the crew doctor but he won't listen to me. He hates doctors."

"Very foolish of him," I agreed. I wanted her on my side. "I saw you at the purser's desk this morning complaining about Lord Fothergill."

"Who?"

"Spike. The Chihuahua."

"Ah. Yes. The one that's now gone missing," Diandra confirmed, popping my toothpaste into a little StarSea bag and presenting the chit for my signature.

"So — you know about that . . . ."

"Word travels fast."

"Did Spike frighten you?"

"Me? No." She pooh-poohed the very idea. "I love animals. All of them. I was a certified dog-walker before I joined the *Sapphire*. I had to do a course."

"Then why were you complaining at the purser's desk?"

Diandra looked at me. "Danny made me do it. He wanted to make a point."

"I understand you were in the vicinity of the Enclosed Prom this morning when Spike disappeared. About 10 a.m."

Diandra looked uncomfortable. "Who said that?"

"You were seen."

"Please don't tell The Dragon Lady."

"I won't mention that you'd stepped away from your post if you tell me what you were doing standing in that doorway."

"One of the passengers forgot his phone and I was trying to see if I could find him to give it back."

"Why not just keep it safe and wait for him to retrace his steps?"

"I don't know," Diandra said. "I thought I could catch him."

"And did you?"

"No. Unfortunately."

"Did you happen to notice Miss Ferryman and Lord Fothergill?"

Diandra thought for a moment. "No."

"Do you have any thoughts about who might have been annoyed enough at the dog to kidnap him?"

Diandra paused. "Ask Danny," she said, handing me the little StarSea bag.

Danny was arranging photos from the welcome aboard dinner on the display racks at the photo gallery across from the Atrium Room.

"How are you feeling?" I asked, stopping in front of an 8 x 10 of Honey and Mitch in their matching turquoise windbreakers, toasting the camera with glasses of wine in one hand and cellphones with pictures of their glasses of wine in the other.

"Better," Danny said. "Thanks."

Some people suffer terribly from motion sickness — my sister is one of them. She can't read in cars or on buses, and if you put her on the water in any kind of conveyance, even if it's calm, you're asking for trouble. Some people are only affected by rougher seas. And some people, like me, seem to be immune to everything. Danny was like my sister. I could have suggested half a dozen other occupations that he'd have been more suited for, on land, but there's no accounting for the spirit of adventure.

"I'm looking into the disappearance of Miss Ferryman's Chihuahua."

"Good riddance, as far as I'm concerned," Danny replied. "He ruined an expensive pair of shoes. Brand new, too."

"I understand you were taking Miss Ferryman's picture this morning roundabout the time the dog disappeared."

"I was taking a lot of pictures of a lot of passengers. It's my job."

"Yes, but you provided enough of a distraction that she didn't notice when she became separated from Lord Fothergill."

"And you think I did that deliberately?"

"It had crossed my mind. And your purchase of seasick tablets just now wouldn't have anything to do with possibly keeping Lord Fothergill sedated and quiet for the duration of this cruise . . . ?"

"Very definitely not," said Danny. "I had nothing to do with that damned dog's disappearance. In spite of what Diandra might have told you."

"Why would she implicate you?"

"I've got no idea," Danny said, as Mitch and Honey approached him, cellphones out. "But if you're looking for someone who really hates dogs, check out the ship's *maître d'*."

I knew Marcello would be busy dealing with lunch. So I went upstairs to Lido and the Outside Prom, where the bottoms of our lifeboats hung overhead and, if you looked down the length of the ship, you were reminded of her past glories as a passenger liner, and not of her current itinerary, cruising in endless circles.

And that was where I spotted it.

A feather.

The feather.

A little worse for wear, having been blown by the wind into a corner occupied by one of the tall wooden lockers that contained our spare lifejackets. But it was purple. And it was Spike's.

And it was on the deck above the deck where he'd last been seen.

If I'd been a forensics expert I'd have bagged it immediately and subjected it to a microscopic examination. Lacking a bag and anything remotely resembling a lab, I picked it up and took it up one more flight of stairs to the Sports Deck, which featured a netted basketball court and tables and chairs at the aft end, and the TopDeck Lounge overlooking the bow. In between was a hinterland off-limits to passengers.

This was where the crew would go to swing the davits out to launch the lifeboats if it became necessary to abandon ship. The *Sapphire,* of course, would be dead in the water if that ever happened. Her engines would be off, her massive twin screws stopped. Here and now, while we were underway and sailing at about 20 knots through the Inside Passage, it was windy and noisy — I was up beside the ventilation shafts and our immense navy-blue funnel.

Again, I wasn't sure what I was looking for. A place in which to hide an annoying Chihuahua? I glanced at the lifeboats, which were mostly the old-fashioned open kind, with a deep hull and a capacity for about 100 occupants squeezed in shoulder-to-shoulder on narrow benches. The *Sapphire* had eight of those — covered over with orange tarps — and another four completely enclosed tenders, for puttering back and forth, ship to shore, when we were anchored in shallow waters. There were also seventy-four inflatables, stacked in various places on the outside decks in white fibreglass barrels.

Even if I'd thought one of the lifeboats would be a logical place to hide a kidnapped dog, I couldn't actually do anything to try and confirm my suspicions. It was too noisy to hear anything except the roar from the funnel and the rush of the wind. And I couldn't easily reach the boats — it would have involved a good deal of clambering and manipulation of mechanisms — something that clearly wasn't detailed in my talent contract (except in dire emergencies).

I debated whether Spike's disappearance might be considered just such an emergency and came to the conclusion that it wouldn't.

Popping the feather into my jacket pocket, I went back down to the Enclosed Prom, the last place Miss Ferryman had been with Lord Fothergill. I wasn't sure what I was looking for. Stray Chihuahua hairs? Random scatological deposits . . . ?

There's an edict all StarSea employees must follow. It's posted in the crew stairways and lifts. We're required to Smile and Always Greet Guests in a Friendly Manner. I did so as I strolled past the steamer chairs and the little gatherings of passengers, intent on trying to spot bears and whales as we cruised past colourful fishing boats and pristine harbours. I even smiled at a visually impaired guest with his seeing-eye dog.

Miss Ferryman was in the Atrium Room, keeping company with an assortment of *petit fours*.

"I need to ask you something," I said.

Miss Ferryman didn't offer me any of her pastries.

"When you saw the shoppie standing in the doorway . . . was it open or shut?"

"Why do you ask?"

"Just curious."

"It was open. Wide open."

"But the shoppie definitely wasn't holding it that way."

"Not at all," said Miss Ferryman. "And I don't see what that has to do with anything."

The door in question was always kept shut while we were underway in order to maintain the ship's climate control. Diandra must have propped it open in order to be standing in the position Miss Ferryman had described. I squatted down at Spike-level and looked around. It was a busy thoroughfare, containing the shopping arcade, the photo gallery, ladies and gents public toilets, a main staircase and two passenger lifts. If Diandra *had* lured Spike away, she would have very quickly had to conceal him somewhere out of sight.

I stood up again and walked across to the Ladies' loo. I

listened at the door, then knocked and waited. Nobody there. I slipped inside and did a quick recon of the two stalls and the sink. The bin that contained used paper towels hadn't been emptied since last night. I did a quick check, just in case. No limp Chihuahuas.

Relieved, I left and walked over to the Gents on the other side of the foyer.

Again, the cleaners hadn't been 'round yet. Because if they had, they'd have noticed the little glass dish on the floor under the sink. I recognized it as belonging to the crew bar. Slightly chipped and with a well-worn StarSea logo in white on its side. And containing the remnants of something dark brown and strongly smelling of malt . . . Guinness.

I found Javier near the Aft Prom hot tub, collecting empty plastic drink tumblers to take back to the pool bar.

"How's business?" I asked. "Looking forward to your disembarkation?"

"Is busy business," Javier replied wearily. "You want drink? I can get you."

"Thank you," I said. "Just a fizzy water, please. With a twist of lime."

He went to fetch it while I sat at a little white plastic table beside the deserted outdoor pool. The Alaska run's not like the Caribbean. It's rarely hot, even at the height of summer. It's breezy and cool and most passengers prefer being boiled alive in the jacuzzi to the temperate chill of the swimming pool.

"You've heard about the disappearance of Lord Fothergill," I checked when Javier returned with my drink.

"The dog?"

"Yes, the dog. The one who made a mess beside the hot tub last night. You had to clear it up."

"Is my job," Javier shrugged.

"Yet you were at the purser's desk this morning to lodge a complaint."

"Was there because chief pool butler say, come with me, we make voice together."

"So you were only there because Peter encouraged you. And you felt nothing bad about the dog?"

"I think about getting off ship and flying home. No think about bad stinking dog."

"I saw you in the TopDeck Lounge last night, buying some Guinness."

"So what? Was late. Nobody there, everyone in bed. Just you playing with yourself. Nobody to complain about deck steward out of uniform in off-limits passenger bar."

"What did you do with the Guinness?"

"Took to cabin. Save for later."

I didn't believe him. You can tell when some people aren't telling the truth, and Javier was like a big see-through picture window. But I didn't have a chance to ask him anything else because his presence was required at another table for drink orders and our guests always took priority.

I collected my fizzy water and went over to Jackson, the drink-slinger behind the pool bar.

"You've been on duty since your shift began?" I asked.

"Since 9 a.m.," Jackson replied. "And I had nothing to do with that dog's disappearance."

I laughed. The entire ship had to know about Spike by now—and about me being asked to investigate.

"Can you just tell me if Javier was here at about 10 a.m.?"

"He was," Jackson confirmed.

"And he didn't leave at all?"

"He's been working solidly for the past couple of hours."

"No pee breaks, nothing."

"Two pee breaks — and he used that one." He nodded at the Gents loo behind the bar.

"Not the toilet near the shopping arcade?"

"Of course not," Jackson said, as if I was daft.

It was time to consult the captain's secretary.

Sal's office was tucked in behind the bridge. It was a storage-cupboard-sized cubbyhole housing the usual business furniture. Sal, who was my age, had made a career out of sailing the seas. She had long dark hair tied back with a big black bow. She was considered an officer — she had tabs on her shoulders — and the ribbon wasn't regulation, but the captain liked her and nobody dared make an issue of it. On that afternoon, she was sorting through the week's start-of-cruise paperwork.

"Let me guess," she said. "You're hot on the trail of the missing Chihuahua. I was just processing the documents for US Public Health. We actually have two support dogs on board this week." She flipped the report around, so that I could have a quick look. "Mr. Chandler. And Ambrose. Quite an interesting story there."

I read the comments from Barrie and Quentin about the fellow with the guide dog I'd encountered during my tour of the Enclosed Prom. Interesting indeed.

"How can I help you with Lord Fothergill?" Sal inquired.

"Do you know who snatched him?"

"Absolutely not."

I believed her. She was — and still is — one of the most honest people I've ever met. Plus, she loved me, which was always a bonus — though we would never have taken our relationship to the next stage. Not while we were both working aboard the same ship, anyway.

"Unless you've made it your business not to know," I said,

after a moment. "Someone mentioned to me that Marcello hates dogs. Might you be able to comment on that? Or anyone else...?"

Sal didn't say anything. She got up and opened the middle drawer in the filing cabinet.

And then had second thoughts as the ship's first officer appeared in the doorway with a request for her to please join the captain on the bridge.

"Crew dockets are confidential," she reminded me over her shoulder as she followed him out.

Afterwards, I reclaimed my steamer chair on Aft Prom. And it was while I was there, keying my thoughts into my phone — along with a group invitation to all my suspects to join me in the *Sapphire's* library at half-past two — that I was visited by Mr. Chandler. And Ambrose.

"Good afternoon," he said.

"'Afternoon," I replied, with my required smile.

"I understand you're looking into the disappearance of a dog."

"The entire ship must know about it by now."

"And most of the internet," Mr. Chandler said, amused. He commandeered an empty chair beside me. "Mind if I join you? It's just that I think I might have some information you might find useful."

I knew we'd be undisturbed in the *Sapphire's* library. Even though it featured computers as well as books in glass-fronted cabinets, comfy armchairs and writing tables, it was one of the least-used places aboard the ship.

I waited for everyone to arrive, and then posted a little

sign that said PRIVATE MEETING on the door and closed it.

There they were: my rogues' gallery. Diandra the shoppie and Danny the photographer. The *Sapphire's maître d'*, Marcello. Chief Purser Barrie and Quentin, his assistant. Samuel, the TopDeck's bartender and Carla, the waitress, and Javier the deck steward and Peter the chief pool butler. Chef Franco, with his legendary short fuse.

And Mr. Bothwell, the passenger with the phobia of dogs.

"Are we expecting ruff seas?" Quentin inquired.

"Murder on the Ketchikan Express?" Samuel quipped.

I smiled.

"You may all be wondering why I've assembled you here," I said. "I believe you may all have some information that will help me solve Lord Fothergill's disappearance."

My guests looked confused.

"Diandra," I said. "I know you were not actually in your shop at 10 a.m. In fact, you were in the foyer near the Promenade door."

"That's right. Yes."

"You told me that you didn't recall seeing Miss Ferryman and Lord Fothergill. But I don't believe you. You couldn't have avoided seeing them. As well as Danny. Would you like to change your statement?"

Diandra looked conflicted.

"Yes," she admitted, finally. "OK. I saw them."

"And what were they doing?"

"Miss Ferryman was having words with Danny. He was trying to take her picture."

"And Miss Ferryman was reluctant to allow him to do so."

"Yes. That's a good way to describe it."

"And while she was preoccupied with Danny . . . what was happening with Lord Fothergill?"

"I already told you . . . I have no idea."

"In fact," I said, "I believe he was investigating the door, which you'd propped open. Am I correct?"

Diandra hesitated. "Yes."

"And do you happen to know why Lord Fothergill was so interested in this propped-open door?"

"Because I offered him a treat. I felt sorry for him! It's ridiculous the way that woman dresses him up in silly clothes. What about his dignity? I just wanted to tell him that I understood how he must have felt, and I wanted to show him a little compassion. I didn't mean any harm."

"And then what happened?"

"He ran off."

"In which direction?"

"Towards the gentlemen's toilets."

"And you didn't think to stop him or go after him?"

"I was . . . distracted."

"By what?"

Diandra looked at Danny. And then: "Not by what. By who. By Marcello."

"And what was Marcello doing to distract you?"

"He was . . . ." She looked down. "Kissing me."

"And was this display of public affection welcomed?"

Diandra paused, and then nodded. "But it wouldn't have been welcomed if you hadn't started secretly dating Carla behind my back," she said to Danny.

"You drove me to it!" Danny objected. "Always going on about my dream of setting up a studio specializing in dog and cat portraits."

"Dogs and cats dressed in stupid outfits in ridiculous poses."

"No worse than wrapping newborns up like Egyptian mummies and pretending they're bumble bees and flower buds — which is what you seem to be obsessed with these days!"

"Let me just clear something up," I interrupted. "Why were you buying seasickness tablets in the shop this morning?"

"I have gastric reflux. That dog aggravated my condition. And I was all out of prescription meds."

"So it wasn't for seasickness at all."

"No. The stuff I was buying is 100 per cent ginger."

"Not the stuff that has Dimenhydrinate in it."

"That only works for nausea and vomiting. Not for what's wrong with me."

"So if you'd wanted to drug Lord Fothergill . . . it would have been completely ineffective."

"Completely," said Danny, glaring at Diandra.

"Thank you."

I turned my attention to Marcello. "I happen to know that you dislike dogs."

"Many people do," Marcello answered diplomatically. "Do you suspect me of an impropriety?"

"Did you abduct Lord Fothergill?"

"No," said Marcello. "I would rather leave it to someone else."

There was laughter in the ship's library.

"Exactly my point," I said. "Can it be that your kissing Diandra was another distraction, to allow someone else the opportunity to do the deed?"

Marcello didn't say anything.

"In fact," I said, "you've requested that you be exempted from duty whenever service dogs are in the dining room. You shouldn't even have been there last night. But the crewmember who should have replaced you was in bed with gastroenteritis. When you were a very young boy, you were given a little puppy, which you adored more than anything else in the world. But you let it out of your sight, and it was trodden on by your careless uncle and was killed. The trauma has affected you ever since. Am I right?"

"Yes," Marcello admitted. "I rarely speak of it."

"Who asked you to distract Diandra?"

"I dare not say."

"Someone who carries some weight aboard this ship," I guessed.

"Certainly not me," Barrie said. "I have a wonderful dog at home, a border collie named Lad. I wish that bloody Lord Fothergill had never come aboard — but I also didn't have anything to do with his disappearance."

"I know you didn't," I said.

"And I hope you don't suspect me either," said Quentin.

"I don't," I said. "I know you'd never risk your position in the purser's office over a contemptuous Chihuahua."

I turned to Javier.

"As for you, Javier . . . you don't drink. You attend the crew meetings of Friends of Bill W and Dr. Bob. Why were you buying Guinness last night? Have you fallen off the wagon?"

Javier looked annoyed. But he was leaving the ship in Juneau and I reckoned I could risk exposing his secret.

Peter, the head pool butler, raised his hand. "He was getting the Guinness for me."

I looked at him. "Why would he need to do that when you can get it yourself from the crew bar?"

"They'd run out."

"I can check that, you know."

"Then do. You'll see I'm telling the truth. I felt like some Guinness and sent Javier to find it. Samuel was very accommodating."

I looked at Samuel. "I do believe you were more than accommodating on this occasion. You also threw in a bottle of Blue Curacao."

Samuel smiled, but didn't say anything.

"I wonder," I said, "who else aboard this ship has a fondness for Blue Curacao?"

I looked at Samuel and Peter and Javier. And then at Carla, who glanced at Chef Franco.

"Ah," I said. "Chef Franco. Whose wife has recently left him for a man who breeds Chihuahuas, and who has been on report more than once since joining the ship for staying in bed and nursing a hangover instead of going to work."

Chef Franco also chose not to reply.

I turned my attention to Mr. Bothwell, who was sitting beside a table that contained a partially-completed jigsaw puzzle.

"You have a phobia of dogs, do you not, Mr. Bothwell?"

"I do."

"I'm sure you had motive and opportunity. But not, alas, the wherewithal. It's difficult to stow a Chihuahua in a passenger cabin. Your steward would have discovered it very quickly . . . unless of course . . . you have him stuffed in the safe."

Diandra gasped. "He'd be dead in minutes!"

"I did not kidnap that dog and stuff it into my safe," Mr. Bothwell said, indignantly. "You're very welcome to go and look."

"That won't be necessary. Do you know where the root of your fear of dogs lies?"

"When I was a newborn I was nearly smothered by a Chihuahua," Mr. Bothwell replied. "I blame my mother for leaving me unattended on the changing table. I'm working with my therapist to recover these hidden, dark memories."

"And your mother, Mr. Bothwell, is . . . ?"

"The wife of Chef Franco," Mr. Bothwell said, after a moment.

"Soon-to-be-former-wife," Chef Franco corrected, spitefully. "Mr. Bothwell, he is my step-son."

"I can confirm that," said Barrie. "He's aboard the ship as a guest of our executive chef."

"And you both despise Chihuahuas . . . as well as Mrs. Franco. So it would not," I said, "be a stretch to suggest that it was Chef Franco who encouraged Marcello to distract Diandra, giving Mr. Bothwell an opportunity to lure Lord Fothergill into the gentlemen's toilets. Where you, Chef Franco, were waiting to ensure he would cause no more disruptions aboard this ship."

"You can prove nothing," Chef Franco declared, standing up.

"Sit down," I said. "I believe I can."

I got up and opened the library door.

"Please come in," I said to Mr. Chandler and Ambrose.

They entered and I led them to a seat as far away from Mr. Bothwell as possible.

"I just want to say that you're not in any trouble, Mr. Chandler. Were you in the gentlemen's toilet near the Atrium Room at about 10 o'clock this morning?"

"I was," Mr. Chandler confirmed.

"And do you recall if there was anyone else in there with you?"

"There was."

"Can you identify that person in this room?"

Mr. Chandler turned his head towards Chef Franco. "Him."

"Impossible," Chef Franco declared. "This man cannot see!"

"In fact," I said, "Mr. Chandler can see perfectly well. It's his dog, Ambrose, who has lost his sight. He was questioned last night after he was spotted by one of the ship's officers leading Ambrose to the sandbox so that he could relieve himself."

"I couldn't leave him at home," Mr. Chandler explained, removing his sunglasses. "He's been with me for fifteen years and he doesn't have much time left. I thought I could just tell a little fib... he is an assistance dog. But I'm the one providing the assistance."

"And can you tell me what you saw in the gentlemen's toilet?" I inquired.

"I saw the little dog with the purple feather, and I saw that man there. And that man there had a bowl filled with something... if I didn't know better I'd have said it was beer... dark beer...."

"Guinness?" I suggested.

"It may have been Guinness."

"Chihuahuas love Guinness," said Diandra.

"Could the Guinness have been used to sedate Lord Fothergill?" I asked.

"I believe so," Diandra said. "Yes."

"Did you see what happened next?" I asked Mr. Chandler.

"I didn't. Ambrose and I left. But that man . . . ." He nodded at Chef Franco. ". . . had a large shopping bag with him."

"I suggest," I said to Chef Franco, "that after you administered the Guinness to Lord Fothergill, you waited in a cubicle until it took effect, after which you popped Lord Fothergill into your shopping bag and spirited him away. Where is he, Chef Franco?"

Chef Franco glared at Mr. Chandler, and then at me, and then at Ambrose. And then he leaped up and made a calculated run for it, sprinting past the sightless dog, yanking the library door open and disappearing down the passenger stairs before I could stop him.

He wasn't going to get far. He obviously couldn't get off the ship. I followed him down, knowing he was running on adrenaline, from the Sports Deck, to Lido, Promenade, Aloha and Baja. That was where he tried to lose me, ducking down narrow corridors that led through the labyrinth of passenger cabins. He didn't count on me knowing more about the *Sapphire's* layout than he did. But he'd only been on the ship for three weeks; I'd been aboard for the whole season.

I was waiting for him by the portside door to the Showcase Lounge — really the only place he could end up, given his trajectory.

All the new ships have their entertainment venues purpose-built. Lovely huge rooms that can accommodate everything from circus acts to water ballets to stage shows direct from Las Vegas. Our little Showcase Lounge was tiny, created out of the ship's original cinema. It had storage space underneath its stage for costumes and props and which, I could confidently state, now secreted a very vocal Chihuahua who, from the aroma surrounding the general area, was also suffering from a very messy case of Guinness-induced diarrhea.

"Are you going to liberate the poor thing," I said to Chef Franco, "or shall I?"

"Take him," Chef Franco said, spitefully, yanking Spike out of his cubbyhole prison and pitching him at me.

I caught him before he could crash to the floor.

With an ungrateful snarl, Spike sank his teeth into my arm.

"*I hate you*," I said, disengaging his mouth and holding his snout closed with my free hand so he couldn't inflict any more damage to my anatomy. "You're lucky a Cocker Spaniel saved me from drowning at the seaside when I was ten. Otherwise, right now, you'd very definitely be sleeping with the orcas."

If Miss Ferryman was at all grateful for Lord Fothergill's return, she had an odd way of letting me know.

"Where is his cardigan?" she demanded, as I handed him over. I'd given him a quick rinse in my cabin, lathered him with my favourite lemon and lime shower gel and fluffed him up with my hairdryer. "And his scarf? And his *feather*?"

"I'm afraid I have no idea," I replied. The scarf and the cardigan had been discretely discarded in triple-wrapped rubbish bags. There was no way I was giving back the feather.

"We are disembarking in Juneau," Miss Ferryman said, full of spite. "And your head office will be hearing from us."

"I'm sorry you feel that way," I said, dismissing her with my best StarSea Customer Service Training Manual smile.

I waited until we'd sailed out of Juneau before I stuck Spike's purple feather in the fretboard of my favourite acoustic guitar, up between the nut and the tuning pegs, where smokers usually jam their ciggies.

"I'd like to dedicate my first song tonight," I said as my audience trickled in, "to a memorable little fellow who brought us all a little closer together this week."

I really needed a banjo and a mandolin and an upright bass to do the tune justice. It was Bluegrass, in the truest sense of the word. But I'd laid down some backing tracks on my magic machine and I could handle the accompaniment with just my Gibson.

"For Spike," I said to a smattering of appreciative laughter. "Salty Dog Blues."

4

COLD WAVE
BY MARCELLE DUBÉ

The ribbon of tracked snow stretched pristine white against a backdrop of black spruce and cold-hardened blue sky. To Olivia's right was a ditch, with the forest looming beyond. On the other side, in the Whitehorse valley far below, wood smoke plumed straight up from chimneys. Not a breath of wind, either in town or up on the trails.

There were other skiers out there today, judging by the number of cars she had left behind in the clubhouse parking lot, but they were keeping to the short loops near the clubhouse. Only she and her friends were brave enough — foolish enough — to take the Bates cross-country ski trail.

In the distance, a snowmobile whined. That was some determined rider. At minus twenty-five Celsius, riding a snowmobile would be like riding a block of ice. In a wind tunnel.

Olivia slowed to a stop, breathing through the merino wool neck warmer, trying to convince herself that she would catch up to her friends soon.

She planted her ski poles in fresh snow and tucked her tufted mittens between her thighs before covering her eyes with her bare hands to melt the ice on her eyelashes. She wiped her eyes and pulled the mittens back on.

Another hour and a half should get her to the cabin. Good thing, too, because she was already starting to lose the light. January days in the Yukon were longer than in the dark depths of December, but they were still short.

The annoying whine of the snowmobile was getting closer. What kind of idiot went snowmobiling in these temperatures?

She grinned under the neck muff. What kind of idiot went *skiing* in these temperatures?

Only lust would bring her to this state.

She had planned to ski to Hudson Hut, near the end of the Bates Trail, with Justin and Caroline, and their friend Leo. Big, beautiful Leo, who said Olivia's name like a caress. The plan was to leave after lunch for a leisurely ski to the hut where they would overnight.

Olivia had been scheduled to work that morning and would meet them at the club house. But work had gone late. She had told Caroline and Justin to go ahead and she would catch up. Lovely Leo had left earlier to start a fire at the cabin and put the hot chocolate on. She couldn't help hoping he was planning some kind of romantic surprise.

But now, as her skis glided on the track and her cold muscles started to warm up again, she wished Caroline and Justin were with her. She glanced at the sun and the rainbow parentheses around it. Sun dogs. Which meant a cold wave was on the way.

This is how people die, her more rational side warned her.

But she was well dressed and well prepared. And Hudson Hut had a big wood stove and lots of split logs for burning. Bunk beds could accommodate up to eight people and they had brought lots of food. Once she got there, she'd be fine.

She hadn't gone thirty seconds before the whine of the snowmobile suddenly sounded louder. She glanced over her shoulder, but the trail disappeared behind a curve.

Was the rider on the *ski* trail? Holy . . . .

She quickly stepped off the trail into the soft snow on the shoulder. She would move off a few feet and wait, to be on the safe side.

Then her leading ski slid into the side of the ditch and she lost her balance, tumbling to the bottom in a flurry of snow.

The snowmobile rounded the curve and sped past her, leaving a stench of burning oil in its wake. Snow landed on her like icing sugar on a cake and she wiped at her eyes with ice-clumped mittens. She sat up in time to glimpse a turquoise snowmobile, a dark jacket and helmet, and then the snowmobile sped away.

The bastard hadn't even slowed down. Jerk hadn't even seen her. Why couldn't these assholes stick to the snowmobile trails? He was probably drunk, or high. There were enough of those yahoos around.

Muttering under her breath, she shifted her weight and repositioned her skis so she could stand up. The backpack kept trying to drag her back down but after a bit of maneuvering, she regained the trail. Snow had crept down her collar but otherwise, she was okay.

The going was no longer smooth. Jerk-face had wrecked the tracks with his snowmobile treads and now she had to ski over the bumps and grooves left behind by the machine.

By the time she reached the hut, it was almost full dark. The cold wave had rolled in as the sun set and Olivia figured it was at least minus thirty. Her feet were lumps of ice in her boots and her hands were chilled, too, in spite of the pair of gloves she had dug out of her pack to slip on under her mittens. Her hat was pulled down to her eyebrows and her neck warmer pulled up over her cheeks.

She was cold, and hungry, and tired. Even her bum was cold, in spite of her insulated ski pants.

The trail kept going past the hut's front door, but she stopped shy of the stoop. The two windows on either side glowed warmly, throwing golden light on the snow below and highlighting the nearby spruce and poplars. A cord of split wood was stacked under overhanging branches a few feet from the hut. She spotted three pairs of skis leaning against the wall by the door, ski poles planted nearby in the snow. The little knot in her chest loosened.

They were here. Of course, they were. Where else would they be?

Then her frozen nose caught a familiar smell. Gasoline and burning oil.

Tucked under the overhanging branches of a spruce tree was a snowmobile. It was hard to make out in the disappearing light, but it looked turquoise.

Lord love a duck — was Jerk-face *here*? Her vision of a romantic couples' weekend evaporated.

At that moment, the door opened, and a tall figure stepped out onto the stoop. With the light behind, she couldn't tell who it was. The figure paused, facing her, and she wondered if he — it had to be a man, at that size — could see her in the near-dark. She kept quiet, hoping to hide the tears that threatened, whether from cold or fatigue — or disappointment at having an unwelcome fifth at their weekend — she didn't know.

"What's the matter?" asked a gruff male voice from inside. She didn't recognize it.

The figure on the stoop turned back to the open doorway. "Nothing. It's a lot colder than it was." It was Leo. His hand was making strange, urgent motions behind his back.

He wanted her to move away from the door.

Her heartbeat spiked and she poled away, passing the snowmobile and heading for the corner of the hut.

"What's taking so long?" asked the gruff voice again, clearer this time, as she was turning the corner. It wasn't Justin.

"Just hold your horses," said Leo. "I'm putting my mitts on."

Then she was around the corner and out of sight.

What was going on? Why was Leo warning her off?

There were no windows on this side of the hut. On the back were three windows, smaller than the ones in the front, but no back door. She skied to the back corner and peered around.

The windows spilled light onto the snow, revealing the solid rectangle of an outhouse and a hole in the forest where the Bates Trail branched off. The side trail climbed for another fifteen minutes to a look-out that revealed the entire Whitehorse Valley, swept past the ski hill at Mount Sima and on to Mount Lorne in the Carcross Valley.

She stopped before the first window. Why had Leo shooed her away? Who was Jerk-face? And why was Leo taking orders from him?

She listened hard, but all she heard was the sound of the door opening and closing again. Leo had gone back inside.

Surely he wouldn't leave her out in the cold without a good reason.

As if conjured by the thought, the cold descended on her like a beast. Whatever Leo was up to, he had better do it quickly before she froze to death.

She undid her ski bindings and rested the skis against the back wall, careful not to make a noise, then crept to the nearest window. It was a little high off the ground, but she tamped down the snow to make a firmer surface and, standing awkwardly on tiptoe, peered in.

The hut consisted of one large room, with a set of double-wide bunk beds at either end. A wood stove stood against the back wall although she couldn't see much of it from her vantage point. She saw Leo bend over with a poker in one hand and a couple of split logs in the other arm. Still wearing his jacket, he stirred the fire and stuffed the logs in.

The light from kerosene lamps on the wall turned his warm dark skin almost lustrous. Luscious Leo indeed, but why was he keeping her from going inside?

The poker was still clenched in his fist, half raised. His tension radiated through the walls.

What the hell . . . ?

Then she spotted Justin and Caroline sitting at the rough-hewn table in the centre of the room. There was a greasy rag at the other end of the table with a small piece of machinery — a spark plug? — resting on top. Justin had dried blood in his fair hair and was staring down at the table while Caroline watched him like a hawk. Her long dark hair was dishevelled and mostly pulled out of the braid at the back of her head.

Their hands were bound behind their backs.

Olivia's mouth fell open beneath the neck warmer.

A strange man suddenly came into view. He must have been standing on the other side of the wood stove. He had a gun in his hand, trained on Leo. He spoke but she couldn't make out the words through the thick glass.

The poker in Leo's hand lifted slightly. Then he glanced at Caroline and Justin, and his hand relaxed. He leaned down, coming perilously close to the window where Olivia stood peering in. He glanced directly at her and shook his head minutely. When he straightened, the poker was no longer in his hand.

Holy . . . .

Olivia turned away from the window and leaned back against the cold log siding. Her mouth felt dry.

They were being held at gunpoint. Justin was hurt. Maybe badly hurt.

What should she do?

There was no cell signal at the hut. There would be none until she was halfway back to the club house.

Was that what Leo wanted her to do? Clearly, he didn't want her to show herself. But she couldn't stay outside, either. Already her hands were tingling.

She looked around the small clearing, frantically trying to think of a way to help her friends. She had no idea what Jerk-face wanted but the fact that he was holding a gun on them did not bode well.

On the other hand, he hadn't shot them yet.

Her gaze fell on the dark hole in the forest where the side trail disappeared. She might get a signal at the lookout.

She grabbed her skis and poles and, crouching to be below the windows, dashed to the far corner of the hut, closest to the trail. Fumbling, she managed to secure her ski boots to the bindings and with a glance at the hut to make sure Jerk-face wasn't staring out the window, she set off for the trail.

Within moments, she could no longer see the hut, or the glow from the windows. She stopped briefly to pull out her cell phone from its inner pocket. It was very cold and, as expected, there was no signal. Reluctantly, she pulled her clothes open until she could slip the phone into her bra, where her body heat would warm it up. It was like sliding frozen metal against her flesh. She tucked herself in and forced herself to move.

The stars were coming out and she was pretty sure the moon would be almost full tonight, but it hadn't risen yet. Still, the trail was visible, pale white between dark palisades of trees.

There was no wind among the trees, thank God, or she would have no chance. As it was, her breath rasped roughly as she pushed herself to go as fast as she could. Despite the neck warmer over her face, the cold attacked the tip of her nose.

With the drop in temperature, the snow had lost a lot of its glide factor and it was a grind to keep going, but she didn't dare stop.

Her breathing grew more ragged as she climbed higher, and her movements slower, but she kept going. Her friends were counting on her. Or at least, Leo was. Justin and Caroline hadn't seen her.

She realized she had reached the top when the trees dropped away on either side. She stopped and turned in a circle. She'd never been here at night.

Below, looking almost close enough to touch, Whitehorse lay nestled in the valley, its lights promising warmth and safety. Wisps of wood smoke rose from chimneys, barely visible in the dark. Beyond the valley, mountains rose like a ghost army surrounding the small city. She could even make out the faint strip of the Yukon River threading its way through.

And above . . . . Above, the stars blazed down at her in a glory of light.

She shook herself and planted her poles in the snow. A faint breeze toyed with the snow-laden branches of the spruce trees. She turned her back to it before removing her mittens and digging through her clothing to finally reach her phone.

Her fingers already stiffening, she clumsily punched in her code. At once the screen cleared to show her icons and she breathed her thanks to the universe. She had bars.

She punched in 911 and hastily slid the phone under her hat and earmuffs. She closed her eyes in relief when the phone rang at the other end. After two rings, someone picked up.

"Nine one one, what is your emergency?" came a woman's voice, as clear as if she were standing next to Olivia.

Olivia pulled down the neck warmer. "I need the police," she said, her words coming out slowly past her stiff lips.

"What is the emergency?" repeated the woman.

Olivia marshalled her thoughts. She hadn't gotten this far in her planning. A part of her hadn't believed this would work.

She was pretty sure her brain was starting to freeze.

"I'm on the Bates Trail," she enunciated carefully. "At the

look-out. My friends are being held at gun point in Hudson Hut. Please. Send help before something happens."

"What's your name?" asked the woman. "Where do you live?"

Olivia gave her the information, though she couldn't see the relevance at the moment.

"Are you in danger?" continued the woman.

"Yes," said Olivia. A giggle threatened to burble out, but she controlled herself, knowing it was incipient hysteria. Or maybe hypothermia. "I'm very cold but I can't go inside. Because of the gun."

"Can you find shelter?" asked the woman. Olivia thought she detected a hint of desperation in her voice.

"The only shelter is the hut," said Olivia firmly.

There was a pause, then the woman said, "I've alerted the RCMP, Olivia. They will be there as soon as they can. In the meantime, stay on the line."

This time, Olivia did laugh, though there wasn't much humour in it.

"I can't," she said. "I'm at the lookout and there's a wind. I can't stay here. I need to descend, but I'll lose the signal. If the RCMP don't get here soon, I'll have to go inside the hut and take my chances."

The pause was even longer. "I understand. Good luck."

Olivia nodded and disconnected. She slid the phone back in her bra and retucked her clothes. She thought again about the contents of her backpack, hoping she would suddenly remember some magical piece of clothing that she had packed at the last minute. But she knew there wasn't. She had opted for a lighter pack to go faster.

To get to Lovely Leo faster.

But she did have a space blanket. And her sleeping bag. If it came to that, she could crawl into the sleeping bag on top of the blanket and wrap it around her. It would help stave off hypothermia.

And maybe prevent freezing to death.

She was slowly angling her skis around to face the trail when a sound penetrated through her earmuffs. She took them off to listen.

A high-pitched whine sounded far below. She turned in the direction of the sound, her breath pluming in front of her. The Bates Trail was hidden among the trees, but a beam of light occasionally lit up the tops of trees as a snowmobile climbed a hill, only to disappear again as it descended.

Olivia's heart leapt with relief. The RCMP!

The moment she thought it, she knew it couldn't be. They wouldn't have had time to mobilize yet.

Some poor schmuck was coming up the trail. It continued past the hut but just long enough to loop back on itself. Whoever was on the snowmobile would want to stop at Hudson Hut to warm up. They would be greeted by a gun and a man not afraid to use it, judging by the blood on Justin's head.

Crap.

Her neck warmer had iced up from the moisture of her breath. She twisted it around then began to ski down.

At first, she couldn't hear the snowmobile over the sound of her harsh breathing but after a while it whined so loudly that people in the valley could probably hear it.

She wasn't going to make it in time.

The pack felt like a block of lead on her back. She could go faster without it. But it contained the sleeping bag. The space blanket. A few granola bars. Frozen water.

Her forehead was so cold she was sure she had frostbite there. Probably on her feet, too.

Gritting her teeth, she pushed harder against the poles, willing herself to go faster.

The high-pitched whine cut out when she was still only

halfway to the hut. She was too late. She would have sobbed if she could have spared the energy.

She kept going, expecting at any moment to hear a gunshot, and finally stopped while she was still in the shadowy opening of the trees. The hut was well lit. Jerk-face walked by a window but she couldn't see her friends. Maybe they were all sitting down at the table.

Or maybe Jerk-face had shot them.

No. No, she would have heard the sound. Sound travelled at minus thirty.

Where was the new arrival? He hadn't kept going — she would have heard that, too.

She shrugged out of her backpack, leaving it at the foot of a tree, then took off her skis. The poles she kept. They might come in handy. Finally, she eased up to the farthest window and peered in.

The first thing she saw was Jerk-face standing across the room, talking to a strange man with his back to her. The man was dressed in a full snow suit but stood in his stocking feet. Jerk-face still had the gun, but he was holding it down by his leg. He held what looked like a scarf against the side of his face. The scarf was covered in blood.

Alarmed, Olivia scanned the room. Justin and Caroline were still at the table, but Justin was slumped over it, his cheek resting against the table surface. Caroline was crying. Where was Leo?

She finally saw a pair of sweat-pant-clad legs sticking out from the lower bunk on the right. He didn't move.

Her heart sank.

Justin was out of commission and so, it would appear, was Leo. She swallowed hard.

You didn't hear any gun shots.

But there were many ways to injure someone.

Was Jerk-face going to hurt the stranger, too?

No, he didn't plan to hurt the man. They were standing close and the stranger was gesticulating angrily. There was a helmet on the floor by the wall. The stranger's helmet.

As if prompted by the thought, the stranger half-turned toward the room. He wasn't as tall as Jerk-face but he was wide and had a full, dark beard and a shock of wild hair.

And he had a gun, too.

He glanced at Justin and Caroline and turned back to Jerk-face.

Olivia dropped to a crouch. What was she supposed to do now? There were *two* men with guns and her friends were helpless. She had no idea how long it would take the cops to get here, if they came at all. Maybe they would think hers had been a crank call.

She had to get those men out of there. She needed a distraction, even if she had to knock on the door and run away.

And she had to move fast before she stopped functioning. She couldn't feel her feet and her hands were almost useless.

She pulled her left hand out of the pole's strap and began flexing it and shaking it, trying to get the circulation flowing again. Then she did the same with the right one.

Finally, she tucked the poles under her arm and, crouching below window level, scuttled around the hut until she was at the front corner.

And there, parked next to Jerk-face's turquoise snowmobile, was another one. This one was bigger, and it was white. Even in the dark she could see it glowing palely under the stars.

She hadn't been on a snowmobile in five years, when an old boyfriend had taken her sledding at the White Pass. It had been exhilarating. And terrifying.

But she had learned how to start the snowmobile — the sled, as her boyfriend had called it.

She walked as quickly as she could to the white snowmobile and studied its dashboard. The writing on the knobs was hard to make out, but the key was in the ignition. Next to it was a round knob with a flat top. She was pretty sure that was the choke. And next to it was a pull cord.

The pull cord gave her pause. Would she have the strength to pull it? Would she even be able to grab it with her frozen hands?

She glanced back at the hut. Jerk-face and the stranger had been standing between the door and the window. As long as they didn't move, she might be able to do this without them seeing her.

Taking a deep breath of the frigid air, she swung one stiff leg over the seat and sat down. It was like sitting on concrete. She could feel the cold seeping through her clothes.

The key turned easily enough, even with her fumbling, mittened hand, but she had to remove the mitten to pull the choke lever out. Immediately the cold attacked her hand in its thin glove. But she couldn't put the mitten back on. She would definitely need fingers for the pull cord. She stuffed the mitten inside her jacket and zipped it back up.

She stood up on the floor boards on either side of the seat, grabbed the pull cord between her fingers, and hauled up. The cord resisted, then pulled up only to return to its spot with a snick that seemed to reverberate against the trees.

Panicked, she looked at the hut, expecting Jerk-face and his friend to come running out, but the door remained closed.

The cord had been easier to pull than she had thought, but the engine still hadn't started.

She went through the steps in her mind, staring down at the instrument panel. Then she noticed a big button above the choke and vaguely remembered having to push it down before the engine would start.

She pushed down and pulled on the cord just as the door to the hut slammed open. A man stumbled out.

The engine roared to life and the man's shout got lost in the sound. As he ran toward her, her right hand reflexively pressed down on the lever.

The sled surged forward, jerking her back. She clung to the handlebars and tried to steer the big machine onto the trail while she scooted up the seat, leaning lower so the miniature windscreen could protect her from the wind.

Then the windscreen shattered, showering her with shards of plexiglass as the sound of a gunshot penetrated past the whine of the engine. Heart threatening to leap from her chest, she glanced back.

Only one man. She didn't need to see the gun to know the bastard was shooting at her.

Part of her wanted to turn the sled around and run him down but her survival instincts kicked in. She scrunched down as low as she could and pressed down on the right-hand lever. The sled practically became airborne. If he shot at her again, she didn't hear it and then it didn't matter because the trail curved, putting trees between herself and the shooter.

After a while, she slowed down. She was almost at the point where the trail curved back on itself. This was as far as she dared go. Whoever had shot at her would come after her to get the machine back. At the same time, she was going to have to hike back through the trees to the hut and didn't want to go too far.

It was a fine balance. If she misjudged, she'd either be shot or she'd freeze to death trying to get to the hut.

She finally stopped, hoping she had enough distance between herself and the shooter. Even if he came after her, it would take him time. She took a minute to pull her mitten out of her jacket and pull it over her gloved hand. Then she tucked the hand under her armpit, trying to warm it up.

The moon was beginning to edge over the top of the trees and stars filled the sky, revealing a long, treed slope that led all the way to the valley. She had to get the sled down that slope.

Swallowing hard, she eased the machine into virgin snow, pointed it down, and rode it partway to the trees. When she figured she was far enough, she turned the sled until it perched parallel to the slope and switched the ignition off. Then she eased off the machine on the upslope side.

She glanced back at the empty trail. Better than she had expected. No one had shot her in the back.

The sled rested precariously on the slope. One good kick and it would topple over.

In the end, it took a lot of kicking and some shoving before the machine finally tipped onto its side. It landed with a soft thud in a small cloud of snow.

It would take a lot of work to right it.

She was turning away to trudge back up to the trail when she remembered the key. Even if they managed to right the sled, they wouldn't be able to start it without the key.

Once she retrieved the key, she considered throwing it as far as she could into the night. With her luck, it would skitter on top of the crust of snow and she'd have to go fetch it. In the end, she slipped it inside the front pocket of her jacket.

The moon finally cleared the tops of the trees, huge and gorgeous, and the slope glowed in its light.

As she glanced back at the sled, she noticed that a panel had popped open at the back of the seat, revealing some kind of shadowy compartment. And on the bright snow below the compartment, something glistened.

She worked her way to the back of the sled and picked up a parcel about the size of a small pot roast, wrapped in clear plastic. Straining to make out what it was, she turned it this way and that and finally realized that the parcel was actually a big freezer bag that sealed at the top. And it was filled with smaller bags that contained pills. Lots of them.

Holy . . . . Drugs. It had to be.

She had no idea what kind of drugs the pills were, but she had her suspicions. Fentanyl was becoming a big problem in the territory. It was big money, so drug dealers were willing to take big risks.

Was that what this was all about? Were those two men drug dealers, and was Hudson Hut where they met to exchange drugs for money?

Now what was she supposed to do? Take the drugs with her? Leave them here for the drug dealer to find?

No. She was damned if she was going to leave them behind. She'd find somewhere to hide them and tell the police when they showed up. If they showed up.

And if the drug dealer ended up killing her? Well, at least he wouldn't have his damned drugs, would he?

She ran her mittened hand inside the compartment but there was nothing else in there. She closed the compartment door. The bastard would have to climb down to the sled to see if his drugs were still there.

Then she turned and looked up at the slope, which seemed impossibly high. Her gaze caught on the tracks she had left getting to the sled.

Her pursuer would have to be blind to miss them.

She began walking, her boots punching through the thin icy crust. Each step was a struggle of pushing one foot through the crust, pulling it up, and then pushing the other foot through.

By the time she reached the top of the slope, she was breathing hard and sweating a little in the killing cold.

It would be so much easier to go back the way she had come and follow the trail to the hut. But she would run into a man with a gun if she did that, and all her efforts would be wasted. No, she would go through the woods and hope the asshole decided to go after the drugs before going after her.

She wanted nothing more than to sit down in the snow and cry.

But Justin, Caroline and Leo needed her, so she kept going.

Moments later, she was in the woods and making her way back toward the hut.

It seemed to take forever, but at last she caught a glimmer of light through the trees. The hut. She stopped at the last trees to take stock. She was at the side of the hut, where there were no windows. She could see a glow of light coming from the front, where the windows were, but as far as she could tell, no one was outside.

No one in their right mind would be outside.

Taking a deep breath, she left the trees behind and stepped into the small cleared area by the side of the hut. She edged over to the wall and crept toward the corner. Her legs were stiff with the cold and she almost tripped over her frozen feet.

Between the moon and the light spilling from the windows by the door, she could see that Jerk-face's sled had its cover tilted up, as if he'd been fiddling with it, and she felt a surge of satisfaction. It wouldn't start. She'd been right — something was wrong with the spark plug on the table.

So what was he doing in there? Waiting for his friend to come back?

The thought spurred her into action. Crouching, she shuffled past the window and the door stoop. Her friends' skis were still leaning against the wall on the other side of the door, along with their ski poles. She had no idea what she had done with hers. She picked up the nearest ski pole and examined it. Yes, the end was pointy enough to do the job.

She tilted her head as a sound reached her. Snowmobile.

Had the drug dealer managed to start the sled? Maybe he'd kept a spare key on himself?

By all the gods of cold and ice, would this nightmare never end?

She grabbed the second pole, looking down to make sure both were in her hand because her hands were so stiff, and swung them against the door, making a feeble clattering sound. She did it again, for good measure, and then flattened herself against the wall by the door.

Just in time, as the door suddenly swung open, revealing Leo in a sweater and his sweatpants. He glanced outside but if he saw her, he gave no indication.

"There's no one," he said over his shoulder. His bulk blocked the doorway.

"I heard something, you lying son of a bitch!" There was a hint of hysteria in Jerk-face's voice. "Get out of the way!"

Leo was shoved out the door, barely managing to stay on his feet. Jerk-face stepped onto the door sill, looking around wildly. He caught sight of Olivia just as she stabbed him with the poles in the middle of his abdomen.

"You bitch!" he screamed and raised his gun.

Then a sound like Armageddon descended on them and all three raised their faces to the sky. A helicopter swooped in from behind the hut, shining a spotlight on the front of the hut.

Jerk-face lifted his free hand to protect his eyes.

Now! thought Olivia and lunged again with the ski poles. At the same time, Leo leapt on Jerk-face, toppling him backwards into the hut.

Olivia scrambled indoors, trying not to get tangled in the squirming limbs. Leo struggled with Jerk-face for the gun. She dropped one pole and placed the tip of the other firmly against Jerk-face's neck. She pressed hard enough to break the skin. He became very, very still.

She pulled her neck warmer down.

"I'm cold," she said. "I'm tired and I'm pissed off. If you don't drop the gun, I'm going to poke a hole in you."

The sound of the gun clunking to the floor was very loud in the sudden silence. Leo grabbed it and jumped to his feet, aiming it at Jerk-face.

Olivia could no longer hear the helicopter. There was nowhere to land on the mountainside. Maybe the pilot had radioed to the RCMP that there was a problem at the hut. Maybe help was coming.

"Get on your stomach," said Olivia. "Hands on your head."

She stepped away so he couldn't grab her legs.

As he complied, she felt a wave of weariness threaten to overwhelm her.

"Are you okay?" asked Leo.

"I don't know," said Olivia. "Can we tie him up?"

Leo nodded toward Caroline and Justin.

"Take the bungee cords off them. That's all there was. That's why he didn't tie me up, too."

For the first time, Olivia noticed the sheen of blood on the side of Leo's face, black against his golden brown skin.

Son of a *bitch*.

Her pole applied a little more pressure to Jerk-face's neck and he grunted in pain.

Leo's head lifted and Olivia turned toward the open door. She had heard it, too. The high whine of a snowmobile engine. She looked at Leo in alarm but then she heard another engine, and then a third.

Thank God. The RCMP had come.

When the police opened Jerk-face's backpack, they found a pile of money — thousands of dollars. And then Olivia remembered the pills, which she had forgotten to hide in the woods, and handed them over.

The cops found the drug smuggler's sled exactly where Olivia had said it would be. They were even able to start it with the key she provided. Then they followed the drug smuggler's tracks downhill to where he had tried to hide in the woods. By then he was so cold that he gave up without a struggle.

While they waited to be taken into town, Olivia and Leo laid Justin out on the table with the help of an RCMP officer who had been left behind with them. With that head wound, they didn't want to move Justin far. Besides, it was easier to examine him there. Justin kept drifting into and out of consciousness. They placed a jacket under his head and a sleeping bag over him to keep him warm.

Caroline was unhurt but in shock, so they placed her under the sleeping bag with her husband.

Leo refused to let Olivia fuss over him. Instead, he removed her hat, earmuffs, mittens, gloves, neck warmer, coat and boots. Then he examined every inch of her exposed flesh for signs of frostbite. When she started shivering, he nodded grimly and pulled the sleeping bag out of his pack. He set it on the lower bunk closest to the fire and unzipped it. Then he tucked her into it and zipped it up before leaving the hut.

The pain of returning circulation in Olivia's hands and feet was so brutal that she actually cried. The constable pretended he didn't see.

Thank goodness Leo wasn't there to see.

The RCMP officer refilled the woodstove and kept the door open to warm up the space faster. He found the ancient kettle that had been left on the floor by the wood stove and dug through the various backpacks until he found water bottles, which he used to fill up the kettle. This he placed on the wood stove.

Leo returned moments later with Olivia's backpack. He pulled out her sleeping bag and opened it, standing in front of the wood stove to warm the bag. Finally, he returned to her and with the officer's help, they lifted Olivia out of the bunk, placed the warmed sleeping bag down and tucked her into it. Then Leo placed the other sleeping bag over her.

Then he lay down next to her and wrapped his arms and legs around her. For the first time in hours, she was blissfully warm.

Just as she was drifting off to sleep, a thought wafted through her hazy brain.

She had never in her life had to work so hard to get a man into bed with her.

5
NEWS ON THE BUCKHORN
BY K.L. ABRAHAMSON

October mist filled our farmyard. The swirls and billows hid the crooked fence posts and the blackened husk of what had, until three weeks ago, been our barn. It was as if the ground fog could remake everything — at least that was what I kept telling myself. But if the soft pillows of fog hid the sharp pines, the skeletal poplars and the dark ribbon of Buckhorn Road beyond, they could hide other things, too. Like wild animals. Or something worse.

I've always been cautious. I don't like taking risks. I hate not being able to control things around me. I hate it worse when I can see exactly what could happen to me or my family and friends and can't do anything about it.

Just yesterday our Samoyed, Rufus, disappeared for a few hours only to return with blood on his white fur. He had a seriously deep gash on his side. Mom said Rufus got in a fight with another dog, but my Grandpa said it looked more like a knife wound. As if someone had stabbed Rufus but couldn't quite finish the job. Mom told Grandpa to keep his theories to himself, but poor Rufus was still at the vet's and some of the sickos on social media were even placing bets about whether he would live or die.

The fog muffled everything. Sounds slithered through the clouds like snakes through rocks. A raven croaked up above. From far down the road came a hunter's gunshot. Something that happened every year around this time. Even though Mom said there were laws about hunting close to the road, in the fall city men from Prince George would cruise the back roads looking for deer and moose.

The morning smelled of wet leaves, but the lingering scent of barn ashes laid an unpleasant char on my tongue. Mist slid under my collar. It placed dead, clammy palms against my face. I pressed back against the door into the kitchen, my heart beating a little too hard. My breath came in short quick gasps as I grasped the door knob. I didn't want to be out here. I wasn't a brave adventurer stepping out into the unknown. I didn't want to be one. I was fourteen and barely surviving in this dangerous world that had already stolen my father. I pulled my down jacket more tightly around me.

"Ellie James, I better darn well hear your footsteps down those stairs. The horses aren't going to feed themselves." Mom's firm voice came through the door. She'd tried kindness to help me deal with my fear. It hadn't helped. Now she was more about tough love.

Mom couldn't do everything, though since Dad died she'd certainly tried. Then Grandpa came to live with us and things just got harder. Guilt sent me stumbling to the edge of the small covered porch. I could do this. I could. Even if Rick Blanchard and his brothers might be waiting to scare me like they'd done so many times before.

Taking a deep, chill breath, I stepped down the three stairs to the gravel driveway and turned toward the yard. A light breeze swirled the fog and a dark figure appeared. I leapt back, a scream tangling in my throat.

"Ellie, girl. That you?" Grandpa stepped closer, materializing into the hunched, wild-haired, grey-whiskered old man I loved. But this morning, he was carrying a rifle.

"Grandpa? What are you doing out here?" I warily eyed the rifle. It was my dad's favourite with the ornately carved stock. It had been locked up in a gun safe in Mom and Dad's bedroom since Grandpa started threatening to hunt down the mugger who had killed my father.

Grandpa slung an arm around my shoulders. "I'm keeping my best girl safe, o' course. I heard rustlers out in the field last night, but they were gone by the time I got out there. I stayed out on patrol to make sure there wasn't any danger when you came out to feed the horses." He grinned down at me. His tired face was grey, which suggested that what he'd said was true. The trouble was, you never knew whether it was truth or some old memory.

Grandpa's memory *was* bad. Mom even suspected he might have accidently burned down our barn with his pipe. But for all his faults, he was a great person to talk to. I'd shared my fears with him many times. Grandpa understood about fear. He'd fought in the Vietnam War and still had the haunted gaze to prove it. But to see him with a rifle . . . .

"I'll keep you company so your mom can get ready for work without us underfoot," he said.

"Sure. But maybe you should leave the rifle at home. We'll need both hands to feed the horses."

He left the rifle leaning beside the front door and we headed toward the corner of the front field, the mist closing in around us.

"Come on! Come on!" I sing-songed out to the herd of eight show horses that were somewhere in the five acres.

Through the fog I heard a snort and horse hooves trotting on hard earth. Then came a high-pitched whinny.

It went on.

And on.

Out in the fog, our prize filly was screaming.

The dead mare's bulk filled the misty morning. Her black coat seemed to suck in what light there was. No longer the prize cutting horse my mother rode to second place in the World Championships. No longer the calm leader of our small herd of show horses. No longer the mother of the promising filly my mother hoped would pay off the debts Dad left us and maybe even build us a replacement barn. No longer the Lone Star we'd called her.

Mom stood across the mare's body from me and the filly, Skipper's Star, that I had finally caught and haltered. She was dressed in her grey trousers and navy blazer, a red flannel jacket thrown hastily over it all. Her hair, neatly twisted back in a bun, had an unusual flyaway look of loose ends as if she, like our lives, was unravelling.

"So," she said to the uniformed RCMP officer beside her. "What happens now?"

"We're going to investigate, Sarah. We've got Ident coming." The cop using Mom's first name was nothing unusual. She was a Prince George probation officer. She was responsible for supervising offenders and recommending sentences for the court. As a result, she knew most of the police — and the criminals — in town.

I glanced up the hill to where the original police car sat with its blue and red lights strobing against the dark hillside. The filly tugged against her lead. The mist was thinning over the tall grass and the short spikes of wild chives. Off to the east the sun was a hard, white eye over the hilltop. The light and heat swept the mist aside here and there, to allow pale blue sky to show. The sun caught on the windows of our closest neighbours, the Blanchards, two fields away. They'd certainly know what had happened. News always travelled on the Buckhorn.

From the road came the sound of raucous male laugher and the school bus rumble that would take my nemeses, the Blanchard boys, to school. Like predators, they knew I was afraid and took pleasure tormenting me in person and on social media. But every morning I swallowed back my fear and went with them. Except today.

"Ident?" I looked up at Grandpa who stood on the other side of Skipper's Star.

"The ones like on T.V. They poke and prod at a body to learn what happened to it."

I looked back at Lone Star, not liking the thought of pokes and prods. She'd been a good mare; gentle and safe. "I thought she was shot."

"Probably. Most likely. I really can't say," the RCMP officer said. He was smooth-cheeked and pale and kept looking at Lone Star in something like fascination and disbelief.

"T'weren't no gunshot. That's a knife wound, I'd say," Grandpa muttered beside me.

The officer shook his head. "It's the other injuries we're concerned about."

He glanced down at the back end of the mare and away.

I shivered at the memory of what I'd seen. Aside from the horrible wound in Lone Star's neck, she was a froth of mutilated flesh where her anus and vagina had once been.

"Maybe your daughter should head up to the house?" the cop said as if I was a six-year-old.

"Ellie, it might be better if you weren't here for this," Mom said with a slow nod in the officer's direction.

"Mom! I found her. I already saw." I had. Grandpa and I had stumbled through the open areas and caught glimpses of the filly running wild. But it was here, in the midst of a willow thicket near the road that we found her mother. I'd lost my bowl of cereal in the grass. I'd wanted to run back to the house and hide under the bed. Instead, I'd had to catch the filly and had sent Grandpa back to the house to tell Mom. Scariest thing I ever did, wandering the field alone.

Shivering, I crossed my arms over my chest. "I'm not going anywhere."

Mom came around Lone Star's body to me. She gave me a hug. "I appreciate you being brave, Ellie. I do. But I need you to take the filly back to the house. She's freaked out enough as it is. Take her back to the other horses and try to get her to eat some grain. Keep her company. Maybe put her in the round corral with Harvey." Harvey being the aging horse who had been my very first ride. With money as tight as it was, I'd been certain Mom would sell him to not have another mouth to feed, but so far she'd drawn the line there. Who'd want to buy a nineteen-year-old horse except a glue factory?

She was right about the filly being freaked out, but . . . .

"But Mom. I really want to know what's going on. Who'd do that kind of thing to Lone Star? It's sick."

She leaned down to me and caught my chin. "You listen to me, Ellie. I do not want you worrying about this. It was likely just a hunter who shot her — you know what it's like in the fall with all the city slickers hunting from their trucks. After she was killed wild animals probably got at her. Coyotes maybe."

"Really?" I lifted my chin toward Lone Star's rear.

"Wolves. Coyotes. Dogs even. Now head back up to the house or the corral at least. Dad, go with her, please."

Unfortunately, Grandpa agreed.

Back at the yard, the horses crowded the fence waiting for the breakfast that I hadn't yet brought them. I put the filly in the round corral made of peeled lodge-pole pine rails and brought Harvey to join her. The filly galloped round the corral, ignoring the grain buckets and water I set out. She kept whinnying, far more upset than the typical young horse was when separated from their mother. But she finally stopped when Harvey rested his head over her back.

They were about as different as two horses could be. Harvey had the thick neck, short legs and straight shoulder of a typical cowboy ranch horse, with a rough dun coat that was ready for winter. Skipper's Star was all long fine legs, angled shoulders and slim lines, with an inky coat still transitioning from baby fur to horse pelt. Not having a barn or the shelter of her mom was going to make the winter hard for her.

But at least she was safe. The comforting scent of horse, oats and alfalfa helped to dispel all the horrible things I'd seen that morning, but my knees still felt weak.

I glanced sideways at Grandpa leaning on the fence beside me, his foot in its old steel-toed work boot resting on the first rail.

"I don't understand who would do this? Who's stupid enough to mistake a horse for a moose or a deer?"

Grandpa shrugged. "Someone not in his right mind. I hate road hunters. A man should get out with his rifle in the mist and the forest. It evens things up a little." His gaze went distant as he looked up at the hills. "I figured I might head out myself today and do a little hunting."

God help us. Grandpa was having more and more difficulty just finding his way home when he went down the road or out in the fields. If he went out in the woods we'd never find him. And then there was the thought of him with a rifle . . . .

How the heck had he gotten Dad's this morning?

I thought of the wound in Lone Star's neck and my stomach twisted.

"Were you out hunting this morning?" I asked as casually as

I could. I dug my fingernails into the faded silver wood rail, not sure how I wanted him to answer.

"Hunting? Sure. Always go hunting at this time of year. Got something, too." Grandpa nodded to himself. "Nice young bull moose'll fill our freezer for the winter."

The air felt like ice. I choked back bile. No way was Grandpa telling the truth. Had he mistaken Lone Star for a moose? Last year he *had* gone hunting at about this time and he *had* bagged a young moose that fed us well all last winter and into the spring. But not this year.

Unless . . . .

My stomach roiled, thinking of that gaping hole in Lone Star's neck and the stricken look on Mom's face. She'd loved that horse. But she loved Grandpa more. If he'd shot Lone Star what would she do?

I — I had to find out who had done this to Lone Star before Grandpa got blamed. The trouble was, I had no idea how to do it.

The filly had settled and the horses had been fed, so I headed back to the house to wait. I took Grandpa with me, planning to lock Dad's rifle away before Mom saw it. She had enough to worry about.

The kitchen light gleamed through the window even though the sun was burning off the mist. Our feet clumped up the three steps to the porch and all my fear and anxiety started to lift.

Until I realized the rifle wasn't where Grandpa had left it.

Had someone taken it or had Mom found it and locked it up? Either way, it complicated things.

Inside, I poured Grandpa a cup of coffee. Then I went to check the gun safe while he fiddled with his cream and sugar.

The gun safe was in the rear of Dad and Mom's closet and it was locked up tight. I knelt on the carpet outside the closet door and keyed in the code Dad had taught me. The green light came on. The safe door clicked open. Dad's rifle rested in its place next to his shotgun and the .22 he'd taught me to shoot on. I sank down on the edge of Mom and Dad's white-quilted bed. Should I tell Mom what Grandpa had said? That I'd found him outside with the rifle?

I wanted to curl up in bed. I wanted none of this to have happened. I wanted my dad alive again. I wanted my old fairy stories where everything came out in a happy ending.

Upstairs Grandpa had turned on the television and I heard the telling squeal of his favourite easy chair. I headed upstairs to my room and flaked out on my small bed set in the alcove of a dormer window. My phone pinged. It was Marie-Claire from school.

"R U all right?" She texted. Apparently news travels fast in school, too.

"U heard." I texted back.

"It's all over social media. What happened?"

What indeed?

"Mare killed. I found her." Shot? Knifed? Half eaten by wild animals? Tears filed my eyes. "I don't want to talk about it." I set my phone down and curled onto my side. The phone pinged but I ignored it. I wasn't going to share my life on line anymore — not after the sicko traffic about Rufus. Now how could I stop Grandpa from being blamed? I rolled onto my back wishing someone would do it for me.

That night after I went to bed, Mom came into my room. Her dark figure was silhouetted by the hall light beyond the door.

"Ellie," she said. "You still awake?"

I sat up.

She shut the door behind her and sank down on the edge of the bed, bringing with her the scent of Irish Spring soap. She caught my hand and squeezed. "I'm sorry about this morning."

"I'm sorry, too, Mom. I know how much Lone Star meant to you."

Weariness radiated off of her. "She was a good mare. I had high hopes for her babies." We both knew orphan foals don't do as well as other young horses.

She drew in a deep breath. "Listen. This morning I found your father's rifle on the porch. Did you take it?"

I swallowed and looked away.

"Grandpa had it." Then I told her what Grandpa had said, how he'd changed his stories.

Mom's shoulders slumped farther, but she gave me a hug and then stood.

"Thank you for telling me." She retreated to the door. "Don't worry about things, Ellie. Have a good sleep and I'll see you in the morning. I love you, you know."

"Love you, too, Mom." As if that changed anything.

The door slid shut and I lay back on my lumpy pillow. My mind whirled with thoughts of Mom's pasted-on smile at dinner. She'd refused to talk about anything to do with Lone Star; had only said that the police were coming with a truck to remove the body for further examination. She was trying to keep everything together, but I could see she was crumbling.

I spent the night caught in horrifying dreams of men in black robes and hoods with too-bright knives shining in the moonlight. I might never set foot outside my room again.

Mom had other ideas and dragged me out of bed for school the next morning. She'd already fed the horses — I suppose she was afraid to send me out alone — and as I choked down porridge Mom finished with her makeup. She was dressed her smartest in a plain navy suit.

"You're dressed up," I said. "Court today, huh?"

She nodded. "A tough case. I'm recommending jail time, so it's likely I'm going to be cross-examined about my pre-sentence report. I'm pretty sure defence counsel and his client won't have liked it." As a probation officer she investigated people who were convicted of a crime to help the judge with sentencing. She fixed a lipstick smudge and grinned at me as if everything was normal. "So, we're all going into town today."

She even had Grandpa up and dressed — much to his displeasure. Mom glossed over his grousing by saying she'd decided it was time for him to try the local memory day program again. The last time he was there he got into a fight with another participant and almost hit one of the staff.

All I could think of was the fact that we were leaving the horses alone. Would we come home to find them all sacrificed?

Mom wouldn't listen to my protests. She drove me as far as the school bus stop, probably figuring that I wouldn't be alone even if my company was the Blanchard boys.

There was more fog this morning, thick enough that the sun was a thin silver gleam above. To either side the pine trees formed dark walls. The school bus stop was simply a wider spot in the road where a few of us had planted lawn chairs to wait in comfort for the bus that was never on time. Of course, the pink plastic lawn chair that I'd brought from the house had quickly been taken over by one of the boys from the Blanchard house.

This morning the chair was empty, but Sonya Christiansen from down the road stood beside it. She was two years older than me and friends with the Blanchards.

Mom peered into the fog and heaved a sigh of relief. "Good. Sonya's here to keep you company."

As if Sonya would ever even talk to me.

Mom checked her watch. Today was clearly an important case.

I clicked the car door open and went to get out.

"Hold on a moment. Will you be all right?" she asked. Her hand gripped my sleeve, but she needed to leave. Getting Grandpa ready had made us late as it was.

"Mom. I'm fine, all right? The bus'll be along in a minute."

And the Blanchard boys — not that the Blanchard boys offered me any protection, but Mom clearly needed to get going. "Really. I'm good. If anything happens, I'll scream so loud you'll hear me in town." I grinned and eased my arm free and climbed out into the cold. I leaned down to her so Sonya wouldn't hear. "Love you, Mom. Have a great day, Grandpa."

He barely harrumphed as I closed the door. And then Mom's tail lights disappeared down the road and there was only the crunch of the gravel under my feet and the sound of my breath to fill the void. I nodded at Sonya, but she ignored me and focused on reading her messages.

It was too quiet. There should be the Blanchard boys' laughter and the sound of vehicles on Buckhorn Road as people headed into town for work.

It was hard to believe Rick Blanchard wasn't in my chair, lording the fact that he'd taken something from me. He'd tried to take other things, too, like getting me alone to feel under my shirt, or squeezing my wrist so hard that I had a bruise. I'd learned to avoid him and his brothers and wore extra padding in my clothes. Not that it helped. He'd simply moved over to social media, spreading rumours that I was easy and posting photos he took of me here or at school with gross captions.

The dun-coloured dirt road faded into the dun-coloured mist. I was tempted to pull out my phone, but instead I sidled from foot to foot to keep warm and listened to the silence, not daring to sit in the chair that by all rights was mine. No wind in the trees. No vehicle on the road except maybe the grind of the school bus in the distance beyond Buckhorn Lake. Nothing stirred in the trees along the road. The air was heavy with moisture and the scent of fallen poplar leaves and wet pine. There was something else, too, a sweet-sour scent that could be the result of autumn wood rot. Or marijuana.

All the little hairs on the back of my neck stood on end. I did a casual three-sixty turn. There was nothing but Sonya, now smoking a cigarette but still on her phone, the trees and a tinkle of water from the small rill below the road. But I was sure I was being watched.

"Boo!" Something large crashed through the brush from across the road, while three more somethings came from behind me.

I clamped down on my scream, but a squeak still escaped. Rick Blanchard hooted in triumph. Sonya doubled over with laughter.

"Did ya hear her? Did ya see her face?" Rick crowed as he circled around me and shot me with his phone. His brothers stood back to give him room.

He stood a full six feet tall and was broad shouldered and muscled. He had blue eyes, a straight nose and a square jaw that you could mistake for handsome if you didn't see it from my vantage. He sneered at me as he draped an arm over Sonya's shoulders.

"I'm surprised you're here. I thought you'd be all cry-faced at home over your dog and your horse."

I went cold at the fact that he knew what had happened, even if I should have known that he would. Had he been involved? I glanced around. His brothers and Sonya usually just followed Rick's lead. This morning, though, Rick's youngest brother, Jim, actually looked uncomfortable.

I drew myself up to my full five-foot-six. "The police are investigating."

"Is that right? Your mom's buddies are investigating. Well my dad's got buddies in the police, too. So, don't go trying to pin this on us."

The rumble of the school bus cut through the mist and I spotted the yellow gleam of its headlights. When the bus came to a squealing, diesel-scented stop I climbed aboard.

On the bumpy ride in to school I considered what Rick had said. News travelled faster than light down Buckhorn Road. Mr.

Blanchard did have friends he could have asked in the RCMP. Once he would have simply called our house or come over to offer help as most country neighbours did. All that had changed after Dad died and Mr. Blanchard suddenly claimed that the best part of our fields were actually his — as if he'd waited until my family was at their weakest before staking his claim. The whole thing was scheduled for a court hearing to sort things out. But the issues between our families were bad enough. I hadn't told Mom about my issues with the Blanchard boys. That was something I could deal with myself. Or not.

Could I really imagine Rick and the others hurting Lone Star?

Trying to answer that question made school seem unreal. Marie Claire, my sole friend, tried to keep me company, but it was hard to be around her. She wanted to know details. I tried to tell her, but her horrified expression shut me down when I suggested the Blanchards might be involved. In class I was so quiet that one of my teachers asked if I was ill and wanted to phone my mom.

I did. I told Mom I didn't feel well and wanted to go home.

Her answer was emphatic "no." Over the line I heard voices in the background talking about risk assessments, warrants and breach of recognizance — whatever they are. She kept putting her hand over the phone while she dealt with the people in her office, but when she came back on she told me to stay at school. I was to wait in the library until she could pick me up. Boring, but safe.

"But Mom, it'll be safer for the horses if someone's home with them. I have my phone. I can call the police if anything happens. Besides, Grandpa needs someone there for him when he comes home."

She said she'd made arrangements for someone to stay with Grandpa at home and I was to do as I was told. I hung up. Clearly, there was no use talking to her.

So I waited until three o'clock and took the bus home anyway. It was an awful ride with Rick right behind me.

When the bus stopped for us, my knees shook so badly I barely managed the climb down to the road. The October light was fading toward dusk as I headed for our driveway. New mist was already forming as Rick leapt down behind me and yelled.

I took off at a run. Down the road. Down the driveway. I fumbled the key in the lock and slammed inside the kitchen. On the way home I'd seen a police car on Buckhorn Road, so they must be keeping an eye on things. I just wished they'd been at the bus stop.

I stood there panting against the door, inhaling the familiar scents of the old porridge pot left in the sink to soak and the pine potpourri Mom preferred. I flipped on all the lights in the house. It didn't help. The house was full of the ticks and creaks of old wood settling. Tree branches tapped windows. The hot water tank gurgled. Each sound sent my heart racing. I wanted to lock myself in my room.

But that was the person I'd always been — a perfect target for bullies like Rick. Well, I couldn't let it keep happening. Maybe if I'd stood up to Rick long before, he wouldn't be able to spook me so easily now. And Mom needed me to be strong more than ever.

I opened the fridge. As usual Mom had left a casserole ready, so I turned the oven on and slid the casserole in. Dinner on. Check. One thing I could do to help Mom.

I pulled plates out of the cupboard to set the table.

Now I needed to feed the horses while I waited for Grandpa. He'd arrive in about half an hour.

Back outside in my jacket, the sun had fallen beyond the horizon. In the gathering gloom of the October afternoon, the door behind me felt solid and safe, but the mist pillowed down the driveway like something out of a horror movie. From the round corral off to my left came the soft snuffles and hoofbeats of Skipper's Star and Harvey. Harvey nickered, a clear reminder that it was their dinnertime.

Sighing, I headed toward the grain shed.

"Come on! Come on!" I sing-songed into the dusk. I filled buckets and carried them to the round corral. The filly and Harvey stuck their noses in the same bucket to eat. It made me smile as I spread their hay and turned around to the field fence.

Usually the other horses would be lined up with their heads hung over the top rail. Tonight they weren't there.

"Come on! Come on!" I called again and strained to hear their hoofbeats as I filled their feed buckets and spread hay.

Finally, the five horses came at a gallop up the hill and stopped to blow steam in my face. They were hot, as if they'd been running for a while. As if something had spooked them.

A chill ran up my back. I looked out past them, into the gathering darkness. The mist hid details like milk film on a glass. I turned back to the horses and patted their necks. Sweat dampened their coats and steam rose off their backs. Something out there had set them running.

A snicker near the round corral froze me solid.

Then I remembered the talking-to I'd given myself earlier.

"Rick Blanchard, you do not scare me. Go home and let the horses eat in peace."

A figure stirred, barely visible through the milky mist. I retreated a step closer to the house.

No.

I was not going to run. I was not going to let him do this to me any longer. I planted my feet and drew myself up taller.

Rick stepped close enough the mist parted around him.

And in the half-light, I saw.

Not Rick.

The man stood about five-foot-eight with gaunt cheeks and light-coloured, chin-length hair. He wore faded jeans and a jean jacket over a tee-shirt that might once have been blue. He advanced a pace and I backed away.

"Wh-who are you? Wh-what do you want?" Rick I'd been prepared for, but not this stranger. A stranger was seriously more serious! I wanted to run, but my muscles had frozen.

"Wh-wh-who are you? Wh-wha-what do you want?" he mimicked.

I wanted my mother, my father, my Grandpa. I wanted to scream, but I was sure that was exactly what he'd love.

"Not exactly a talker like your mother, are you? Nice and young. Young enough that bitch'll live a life of regret after I'm done with you." He chuckled. A shift of his right hand and the light from the house caught on a blade. Long. Sharp.

Sharp enough it could have stabbed Lone Star in the neck.

He took another step and suddenly my legs were free.

I spun. I ran.

He came after me, but fear gave me speed. I was at the door and up and inside, slammed the door as he stumbled up the stairs. Stabbed the lock shut as he rattled the knob. Hands shaking, I turned to see his face pressed against the kitchen window over the sink. He stabbed his knife at the frame, trying to jimmy it open.

The windows were old, just like the house. He could break the glass. There was no way he wasn't going to get in. I plunged out of the kitchen-family room and into the hall. I needed someplace to hide. Someplace I could call for help.

My room? Hide under my bed? That'd be one of the first places he'd look.

I plunged down the stairs to Mom and Dad's bedroom. The room was dark. It smelled faintly of Mom's perfume and Dad's old cologne. Where to hide and, even if I hid, how long could I stay hidden?

I fumbled out my cell phone and called 911.

A crash upstairs and I dropped my phone. He was coming

through the glass like I'd known he would. I scrambled for the phone and picked it up.

"Police, fire and ambulance. What is your emergency?"

"Th-there's someone in the house. He has a knife."

Upstairs there was another crash as the dishes by the sink were swept onto the floor.

"What's your name?"

"I'm Ellie James. I live on Buckhorn Road. My mother's Sarah James, the probation officer."

Footsteps shifted across the floor upstairs.

"What's your address?"

I didn't dare answer.

Breaking the connection, I backed across the room. Overhead, footsteps came into the hallway. Would he choose up or down?

The first steps came down the stairwell and it was as if everything went still in the room, or maybe it was inside me. I needed a weapon. I knew what to do.

When my father was alive, he used to take me hunting. Mom had hated it and after he died had made me promise I'd never touch one of his guns again. I hadn't.

I stuck the phone in my pocket. As quiet as possible I backed into Mom and Dad's closet and pulled the door closed. I wormed my way to the rear corner and the weapon safe.

Fingers shaking, I stabbed in the code.

The safe lights flickered but the safe didn't beep open. I froze. Had Mom changed the code or had I mis-punched it?

I felt, rather than heard the man as he entered Mom's bedroom. It was like an angry heat came off of him. My fingers shook harder.

"You under here?" he said and I knew he looked under the bed. The closet would be next. I had to have the rifle.

I stabbed in the numbers again but the safe didn't beep.

Please, Mom! You wouldn't change the code. You wouldn't do that to me!

Footsteps padded on the carpeted floor near the closet. I cowered back and tried the buttons once more. Another flicker of lights and nothing.

From outside came the rumble of a vehicle down our driveway. Had the police arrived already? Then there were voices. Grandpa, saying goodnight to whoever had brought him home — probably the person who was supposed to be staying with him. Someone tried the kitchen doorknob and then there was a knock on the door.

I froze. So did the man at the closet door. His footfall quietly retreated to the stairs and started up. The kitchen door opened.

"You can go," Grandpa's voice carried down the stairs. "See, I have my own key. I don't need a babysitter, regardless of what my daughter said."

Please let him see the broken window. Please let him see the glass on the floor. If he did, he'd know there was trouble and so would the driver.

"I'm not supposed to leave you unless someone is home," a muffled voice said.

"My granddaughter is probably just out feeding the horses. Now go on with ya." The kitchen door closed.

The man with the knife would kill them if I didn't do something.

I pulled out my phone and used the glow of the screen to stab in the code one more time. This time the red, yellow and green lights flickered and then the green light flicked on. The safe beeped softly and I yanked open the door. Inside, Dad's rifle lay in its cradle next to the other long guns. He'd always said it was the best weapon around. I checked whether it was loaded and found the ammo in a box on the weapon safe's floor. Fingers shaking, I loaded the chamber and quietly closed the rifle. Then I stood, took a deep breath and shoved open the door.

Outside a vehicle engine flared to life. The driver was leaving.

Grandpa's heavy footfall crossed into the family room and his favourite chair groaned like always. He hadn't noticed the broken dishes or the draft from the broken window. He would turn on the T.V. and be fixing his pipe, leaving his back exposed to the hallway and stairs. The man could slit his throat faster than Grandpa could move.

Knees shaking and palms damp, I crossed to the bedroom door and checked the stairs. No one was there. I pictured the man creeping down the hall toward Grandpa.

Fighting the shaking, I slowly, slowly climbed the stairs. At the top, the luscious scent of Mom's casserole almost turned my stomach, its safe, familiar smell too foreign to the danger we were in. No one was in the hall.

Was the man about to kill Grandpa or had he climbed the stairs to my room to hide? Maybe he'd snuck past Grandpa into the kitchen and out the door to hurt more of the horses. I thought of Lone Star's filly and Harvey trapped in the round corral.

Grandpa came first.

I crept down the hall.

The man stood behind Grandpa's chair, the knife raised in his hand.

"No!" I shouted and leapt into the room.

The man was fast. He grabbed Grandpa's arm, ripped him out of his chair. He held Grandpa hostage in a choke hold. Grandpa's half-lit pipe spun off across the room.

The man's pale eyes glared at me. "Put down the gun, little girl. Maybe I won't slit this old man's throat."

No way. No how. Tears in my eye made it hard to see. My hands shook so hard I'd likely miss any shot. But he didn't know that.

I kept the rifle raised.

Grandpa's wild gaze caught mine. Maybe not so wild. In fact, his gaze was solid. He held my attention as he slightly shook his head. As if he had confidence in me. As if we could do this together.

I nodded, swallowed and aimed.

"No," I said and lifted the rifle barrel a little higher.

Grandpa's booted foot stomped down on the man's sneakered instep. He drove an elbow into the man's midriff and yanked free. The man lunged after him, but not fast enough. My finger tightened on the rifle trigger.

The weapon bucked. The smell of gunpowder filled the room. A crimson blossom formed on the man's jean jacket. He sagged to the floor.

Grandpa stepped between the man and me. Blood streamed down his neck.

The man had cut him! He'd tried to kill him just as he'd killed Lone Star! Just as he'd tried to kill me!

Hands suddenly steady, I stepped past Grandpa and turned the rifle back on the injured man. I wasn't going to let him do anything again. I took careful aim.

Grandpa caught the rifle barrel and pushed it away.

"No, Ellie. It's bad enough what you've had to do. I'm a soldier, remember. I know what it's like to kill a man. You don't want that kind of memory, you brave, brave girl."

From out in the misty night came the sound of sirens. Tires sprayed gravel down our driveway.

I lowered the gun and clicked the safety on. Then Dad's rifle slipped right out of my hands. It thunked on the carpet. Grandpa pulled me into a hug as the door thudded open. Uniformed RCMP officers flooded in.

I don't remember much after that, other than how tired I was. I slumped down on the couch. Grandpa sat beside me.

The police took control of the scene and of Dad's gun. There were ambulances and people and too many questions. Then there was Mom, sobbing as she pulled me and Grandpa into a family hug.

It turned out that the man who had threatened us was none other than the man who was up for sentencing today. After the man's lawyer let the man read Mom's report, he didn't show up for sentencing. The police had been looking for him. They'd even checked here.

The next morning, when I stepped outside onto the porch to feed the horses, sunlight made the mist glow more brilliantly than I'd ever noticed. Down at the round corral, beads of water were crystal prisms on blades of grass and fence posts. The sun burned through the top of the mist so our land fell away in rolling acres of shimmering cloud.

"Come on. Come on," I called and heard the thunder of hooves. The fog roiled and five horses appeared, heads tossing. They settled at the fence for their feed and young Skipper's Star actually nickered for me when I brought her and Harvey's grain.

I left the horses, had breakfast and, surprising even to me, I got ready for school. It felt like a shorter walk to the school bus stop than usual. I looked around and then sat in the pink plastic chair. Then I waited for Rick and the others to show.

They appeared out of the mist like four lumbering beasts — creatures from long ago with Sonya following in their wake. Bullies who'd tormented me. But I'd faced something far worse and I'd won. I gripped the arms of the plastic seat and held on.

The funny thing was, Rick didn't say a thing. He just nodded in my direction and left me alone. He and his brothers stood away from me and talked quietly amongst themselves.

Maybe they'd heard what I'd almost done.

Like I said, news travels fast on the Buckhorn.

6

AUTUMN IS A TIME FOR DYING
BY MERRILEE ROBSON

A woman screamed. Constable Frank Stuart raced out of the Royal Northwest Mounted Police detachment as a man's voice, the words slurred, drowned hers out.

A small crowd had gathered in front of the village store, where a man swayed on his feet beside a woman sprawled on the wooden sidewalk.

Frank squinted as his eyes adjusted to the bright daylight. It was Joe Simmons, of course. The smell of whisky hit Frank as he stepped in front of Simmons and reached down to help the woman to her feet.

The skin around one of her eyes was already darkening. She touched her split lip and blood stained the finger of her glove, highlighting the neat stitches where it had been mended. He quickly offered his handkerchief.

But she ignored it, peering past him at Simmons.

"How could you?" she yelled. "How could you waste my money on liquor? I need it for our children!"

Frank shifted to put himself between the couple in case Simmons tried to strike the woman again. Two men moved forward with the same thought. But Simmons only stared at her.

Then he leaned back against the wall of the shop and slid slowly to the ground.

Two horses, hitched to a nearby wagon, shifted nervously as the crowd around them grew. More people spilled out of the handful of businesses scattered along the small main street that stretched out from the railway station. Frank could see a lace curtain twitch in one of the neighbouring clapboard houses.

He coughed at the dust the horses had stirred up. The rain a few weeks ago had protected the crops from the drought that everyone had feared. But Frank wondered if he would ever get used to the dry air here on the Prairies, so different from back home in England.

"Are you all right, Mrs. Simmons?" Frank asked. "I could call for the doctor. And shall I arrest him?"

The woman shrugged, wincing a little at the movement. "It's not the first time my husband has hit me."

"I can charge him with public drunkenness. You wouldn't need to be involved."

"If you had arrested him earlier, before he spent all my egg money, that would have been a help. Now it's too late. I wanted to buy some flannel, and some wool, to make new winter clothes for the children. Our boy's shot up almost foot since last winter and our daughter's grown too. Now what am I supposed to do?

"I suppose I deserved it," she added, wiping more blood from her lip "I hit him first. No man will put up with that."

Frank frowned. He was sure he would never hit a woman, no matter how provoked. But other men felt differently. Keeping Simmons in the cell might be safer for his wife but, then again, he might batter her even worse when he got out.

"No, I'll take him home," Mrs. Simmons said, "if you'll help me get him in the wagon. He'll likely sleep it off awhile now." Indeed, her husband, who had been so aggressive only moments ago, was curled up on the walkway in front of the store, snoring loudly.

Frank eyed Mrs. Simmons. She must have been beautiful at one time. Her thick, dark hair had some curl to it, if he could judge from the several strands escaping from their pins. Her eyes were dark too, with thick lashes that swept her cheeks as she glanced down at her husband. Her face was weathered, and a scar on her forehead had likely come from a blow like the one that bloodied her lips now. But the face was a perfect oval, framed beautifully by her dark hair.

The woman's hat was lying in the street, not yet trampled by any traffic. He picked it up, dusting the brim and the dark ribbon circling the crown before handing it to Mrs. Simmons. Her white cotton shirtwaist was stained with drops of blood and she was certainly going to have a black eye, but she seemed otherwise uninjured. She appeared angry but not afraid. But would she really be safe?

"I heard your son was talking of enlisting. Is he still at home?"

Mrs. Simmons' injured mouth curved into a small smile. "Our Joseph, yes. He's been talking about it. But why boys from Saskatchewan should care about what's happening in Europe is beyond me. Besides, he's only sixteen. I've told him they won't want a boy. So, yes, he's still at home."

Frank relaxed a little. The boy was still young, but he was surely big enough to protect his mother if his father became violent again. So he let them go.

"Joe Simmons is dead."

Dr. Fletcher had thrown open the door to the detachment and was silhouetted against the bright late-afternoon light.

He closed the door of the small wooden building that housed the detachment and the room immediately filled with a sharp citrus scent. Frank managed to avoid wrinkling his nose. He wasn't sure if it was cologne or hair pomade, but he hoped the smell wouldn't seep into his sleeping quarters behind the office.

"I take it you're here because you don't think it was illness or an accident."

"Well, it was bound to happen sometime, with the amount the man drank. But that's what I wanted to talk to you about," the doctor said.

Dr. Fletcher, uninvited, took the other chair. The office always seemed cramped when more than one person occupied the space outside the iron bars of the cell that took up most of the room. Frank eyed the doctor's tan checked suit with distaste. It hardly seemed appropriate garb to be making medical calls in, let alone announcing a death.

"It would appear," the doctor continued, "that he drank too much of a particularly bad batch of that rotgut whisky he wastes all his money on. He was vomiting and I suspect his heart finally gave out. But it does seem a bit convenient, considering his wife still has a black eye from that fight a few days ago."

"She seemed to think that fight was nothing unusual," Frank said. "But do you think he might have been killed? Is that why you're here?"

The doctor shrugged. "It was probably the drink. Some of that homemade stuff is pure poison. I just thought I should mention it."

"I'll have to find out where the man bought his liquor." A visit to the farm to see if the widow had any idea about that would be awkward, but he needed to do it. "I'll have to check if they need help with the farm, in any case, with her husband dead."

The doctor brushed an almost invisible speck of dust from the cuff of his suit jacket, making it clear that he couldn't be expected to offer help on the farm. "They might appreciate that. Although, from what I saw of the fellow, he wasn't a lot of help. I shouldn't say it, but they'll likely be better off without him."

Frank pondered that comment as he saddled his horse and headed to the Simmons farm. It was true that the death was not unexpected. He'd often thought the man might pass out and freeze to death in a snowdrift or fall under the wheels of a farm wagon. So it wasn't surprising that Joe Simmons was dead. But something bothered him. A niggling worry about the timing, like an itch at the nape of his neck, a coldness when he thought about it.

If he hadn't been fretting about how Simmons had died, he would have enjoyed the ride. The sky was a bright blue and the afternoon still held some warmth. The farmers had made good progress in getting their crops in but the grain still in the fields was golden in the afternoon light. It matched the colour of the birch and aspen making glowing punctuation marks against the almost black of the evergreens. His horse seemed to be enjoying himself, picking his feet up high and creating soft puffs of dust as his hooves left their marks in the road.

But Frank's thoughts were troubled, both by the suddenness of Simmons' death, and by worry about the war that had been going on for almost two months now. He'd asked about joining the expeditionary force that was heading to Europe, but he was told he was needed here in Saskatchewan. And clearly, he was. Fights had broken out between farmers from Britain and their neighbours from Germany and Austria-Hungary, even those who had lived side by side for years. People worried about spies and enemy agents. Everyone was on edge, even though the latest reports from France seemed positive.

But if boys who had been born in Saskatchewan and had never been to England were eager to go off and fight, then why wasn't he doing his part to defend his former home?

The Simmons farm was neat, he thought, as he dismounted and tied his horse to the post. The man might have been a drunk, but someone had painted the house a clean white. Winter vegetables stood in tidy rows in the kitchen garden. Many farmers in the area were content to use their land solely for crops and vegetables, leaving their house fronted only by a bare yard where chickens scratched and pecked. Here someone had devoted time and space to a flower garden.

And not just any flower garden; it was an abundant one, blossoming in a glorious mix of colours that were certainly carefully planned. The late roses and the deep purple spikes of monkshood brought to mind the gardens back home, where gentle rain made flowers bloom almost on their own.

He'd dreamed of having his own garden, but that had been out of his reach in England. And his hopes of having his own piece of land here had been crushed by his few years of homesteading. He had underestimated the back-breaking work involved in clearing land, building a homestead and growing a crop. He'd even had to hire himself out to another farmer to earn enough money to survive the winter. It was hardly what he'd hoped for when he learned there was land available for settlers in Canada.

He knew he was better off with his current post, but he still stared for a moment at the bright flowers, yearning for the garden he had dreamed of.

Here, even in the Prairie climate he found so harsh, someone had made sure they had beauty, as well as the necessities of life. Someone cared enough to spend precious time, space and energy to grow flowers.

There was a spot in the far corner of the garden where the soil was disturbed, with dry stalks of broken flowers littered across rough clumps of dirt.

He frowned. An uprooted rose bush, its branches crushed and cracked, lay on its side. The leaves were already dried and wrinkled but a few blooms left startling spots of crimson on the dusty earth.

He looked from the destruction of that one corner to the healthy green plants and tapestry of bright colours in the rest of the garden.

Whatever the reason for the damage, Frank couldn't bear to leave the rose like that. He bent down, scraping a hole in the earth with his hands and pushing the soil firmly around the damaged roots. His horse raised its head as he walked over to retrieve his canteen from the saddle bag but quickly went back to eating the grass on the verge.

Frank emptied his canteen around the broken rose, wondering if it was a useless waste of drinking water but glad he had done it anyway.

As Mrs. Simmons answered his knock and invited him in, he saw the beauty in the house matched the garden, with bright cushions, a rag rug on the floor, and a vase of flowers filling the room with splashes of colour.

He considered the woman in front of him. Her clothes were worn, and her hands were rough and red. Her eye was badly swollen and had turned a dark purple, darker than the spikes of monkshood in the vase beside her. She looked weary. No doubt she had enough work to occupy all the hours of the day, and more. And yet, she had taken the time to make her home beautiful.

Frank almost complimented her on the room and then remembered in time why he was there. It wasn't the time or the place to discuss gardening and homemaking. He had questions to ask but it seemed rude to start with them right away.

"I wanted to offer my condolences to you and your children," he said, finally, "and to see if you need some help with the farm."

"That's kind of you, but we are used to running the farm on our own. We will manage."

The house seemed silent. "Are the young people doing their chores?" he asked. "Perhaps I could give them a hand?"

"I sent them to school. There didn't seem much point in their staying home. They'll be back soon."

Certainly not the usual mourning practice but carrying on as normal might have given some comfort to them.

"I don't know if your neighbours will have heard," Frank said. "I could ask some of the women to come and keep you company."

"A lot of them never wanted much to do with us. But Mrs. Duncan helped me lay him out. She's always been very kind."

Frank knew he ought to ask to see the body. It would be required for his report. But he hesitated to ask the widow. "I'd like to pay my respects," he said, finally.

She led him to a bedroom where the body of Joe Simmons lay stretched out neatly on a double bed. He was dressed in his best suit.

"The coffin should be here this afternoon," Mrs. Simmons said.

The women had done a good job of the laying out. Frank thought Simmons looked better in death than he had ever seen him looking in life.

"Our Joseph went for the doctor when his father took sick," Mrs. Simmons said. "Mr. Simmons has been bad before, but never that bad."

"Do you know where he was getting the whisky?" Frank asked. "If someone is making it locally, I'll have to stop them, particularly if this is such a bad batch."

"If I'd known where he was getting it, I would have tried to stop him from wasting our money on it!" the woman said. "He was secretive about it. I would think he was working in the field and, the next thing I knew, he had sneaked away."

"The doctor told me he was vomiting." Frank said. He looked around the room, which was clean and neat.

"I cleaned him up and washed everything," the widow said

with an acerbic tone, as if she knew he was thinking of evidence. "What kind of a housewife do you think I am?"

Frank glanced at the body. The doctor's report had said there was no sign of injury and he could see no marks on the man's face or hands. So the death wasn't due to a drunken fight or a beating.

There could be plenty of poisonous things on a farm. But Frank couldn't see why someone would poison him now when he'd been a drunk for so many years.

No, the alcohol seemed the obvious cause of death. He would do his best to find where Simmons had been getting his liquor. And he would write it up as an accidental death, or an illness.

As he left the bedroom, two young people entered the house. The boy was already taller and broader across the shoulders than his father had been. And the girl had the beauty he had seen, almost hidden by the beatings and hard work, in her mother. This girl could likely take her pick from the local lads. Her eyes were as large and dark as her mother's. They reminded him of the eyes of a young mare he had been allowed to ride when he was a boy, one summer when he worked at a neighbour's farm. A mare that had a fine spirit and seemed to know her own worth, as this girl did.

Frank was sure you weren't supposed to compare a pretty woman to a horse. Like a doe or a fawn, he thought. That's how they might describe her in a book. That was somehow more poetic. But the girl's hair shone like the glossy coat of a horse that was well cared for, and she stepped as lightly as the little horse had done. He didn't think it was wrong to compare the two.

The two young people greeted him politely and went through to the kitchen.

As he turned to say goodbye to Mrs. Simmons, his eye caught the vase of monkshood.

There was something about monkshood, he remembered

from the small garden his mother kept at home. He'd always liked the look of the flowers, but his mother hadn't wanted them in her garden.

As he looked back at Mrs. Simmons, he thought he saw a faint shadow cross her face.

"The vase was my mother's," Mrs. Simmons said. "Most of her things were sold, for the farm, or for drink, more often. But I still have that."

The vase was opalescent in the fading afternoon sunlight. She moved it slightly so the glass caught more light and glowed.

"She didn't want me to marry him," she said, casting a glance back at the bedroom where her husband lay. "She said I could do better. But I was so in love and so headstrong. I've a girl like that, but I hope she makes a better choice."

Frank looked again at the vase. The woman must have come from a more prosperous home, if the family could afford beautiful things like this. The light from the window showed off the swirling colours of the vase and shone through the thin purple petals so they glowed like coloured glass themselves. He almost reached out to touch them. And then he remembered.

The plants were poisonous and the poison from the monkshood stems would soak into the water.

She was silent, seeming not even to breathe as she tried to judge if he knew. Her one good eye gave him a pleading look.

Would it hurt to let it be? Frank wondered if it would be such a wrong to leave this small family together and at peace.

But no, he had sworn to uphold the law. And murder was against the law.

"My ride left me thirsty," he said, "I was going to ask you for a glass of water, but I'll just take a sip of this."

How far could he go with this? Could he just pretend to take a drink? He lifted the vase to his mouth.

Mrs. Simmons held out her hand to stop him. "And yet you used your whole canteen on that rosebush," she said.

"You saw that? I thought it might be saved," Frank said. He still held the vase but lowered it a little. "What happened there?"

She sighed. "What always happens. He said I was always on at him about spending money on whisky. But I was wasting time and space on flowers, when the land could be used for crops. He said he was going to dig up my garden so he could plant a winter crop that would earn something."

"But...."

"I know, it's far too late to plant anything. But he never finished digging up the garden anyway. That was always the way with him. He only ruined the one rose bush and a few of the Michaelmas daisies. And it was such a pretty rose. I don't know why he would want to hurt it.

"You can put that down," she said, sighing. "I'll tell you. I mixed that water with Mr. Simmons' whisky. It seemed fitting."

"But it wasn't about the flowers, was it?"

There were tears in her eyes. "No, I was used to him ruining my things when he'd been drinking. It wasn't the rose."

She looked back towards the kitchen. "Our Mary's caught the attention of several young men. But I've seen the way their mothers look at her shabby clothes. None of them will want their son to marry the daughter of the town drunk."

She smiled. "She's beautiful, isn't she? I saw how you looked at her. I was saving up the money I made from selling eggs and vegetables. Joseph's grown so much he really needs some new winter clothes. But I wanted Mary to have something special. There's some cloth in a dark rose colour that would suit her colouring. I want her to be able to hold her head up. I want her to have some happiness."

Mrs. Simmons sighed again. "But that's not it either. I could have made up that money somehow. I needed to do something about young Joseph. He kept talking about the war. I knew, if he went, he wouldn't come back."

He wanted to argue with her, say she couldn't possibly know something like that.

But she went on. "Don't ask me how I knew it. I just knew it. I could feel it in my bones." She looked in the direction of the kitchen. "Now he'll be safe. He'll have to stay at home to help his widowed mother and sister." She turned back to Frank. "Well, his sister anyway. Don't worry. I won't make a fuss. I'll come with you. Just let me say goodbye to them."

Frank watched as the mother embraced the two dark-haired youngsters. He looked around the lovely room, where she had tried to make a home for her family, despite her husband. She might not have been happy, but she had been willing to accept her life as it was, at least planning for her children to have a happier life. Until the war made that impossible.

Frank wished he could argue with her, that he could turn back the clock to before she had taken that dreadful step.

"They say it will be over by Christmas," he wanted to tell her.

7
A MIDWINTER NIGHT'S SCREAM
BY J.E. BARNARD

Away down the moon-kissed hill, Christmas lights dappled the snowy fields and vineyards. Red and blue lights danced across the dark Okanagan waters. Three vehicles, speeding in close succession, swung uphill onto the first narrow switchback that would bring them, eventually, to us.

"The moon, like unto a silver bow," Steve murmured beside me.

"Stop quoting Shakespeare," I snapped. "Those are cops and paramedics' lights, not Queen Titania's fairies."

"It's a tragedy," he agreed, "not a comedy."

The lead cruiser's lights spun on an icy bend and slid nose-first into a ditch. The second cruiser clipped the jutting bumper and lurched the other way, its headlights swathing the slope below. Another moon quote might have been hovering on Steve's tongue, but he didn't give it voice. Even ex-Shakespearean professors can sense when the audience isn't with them. Down below, the ambulance lights whirled slowly, helplessly, behind the disabled cruisers. Just like that, the only road up was blocked.

"Or a farce," he amended. "Midsummer Night's Dream fits

despite the snow. Which of our guests will take the part of bumbling Bottom, and who will be the Wall, obstructing the investigation?"

"That's more Midsomer Murder than Midsummer Night." I glanced at the terrace where seven writers huddled by the patio doors. "The business won't survive if the guests all give us terrible reviews."

"I'll ply them with tea and honeyed words." He crunched away down the short gravel path, leaving me to guard the mess.

Huddling my dressing gown tighter at my throat, I edged into the dubious windbreak of the latticed fence. The hot tub's steamy halo softened the Christmas lights' glimmer, but it couldn't dilute the horrid reality of our ex-guest's battered torso, face down in the swirling waters. Corpses were as common in my nursing career as sonnets were in Steve's work, but this was the first dead body to threaten our retirement business. We'd be savaged by the press unless I could find some clue to make this not our fault.

Steeling myself, I surveyed the body. Pink-tinged foam gathered in its hair. The exposed torso sprawled from the tub's edge, purple bruises staining the pasty ribcage. One leg hung limp to the wooden deck. The other dangled at waist height, its ankle festively wrapped in tinsel and Christmas lights half unstrung from the fence.

To my crime-show trained eyes, the scene looked staged, but Steve's most post-modern production of The Bard had never achieved this degree of bizarre. Those Christmas lights had been securely tied to that fence a couple of hours ago. No mischievous Puck had torn them loose and strung them across the path. Nor could simply tripping over the string account for that purple ribcage or the bloody seepage around the head. Spend enough Saturday nights working Emergency and you can tell when someone's had the stuffing beat out of them. No way to pretty this up. It was murder.

The tub's motor cut out, leaving a profound silence. Somewhere up the hill, a coyote howled its desolation to the remote and uncaring stars. I knew just how it felt.

30-SOME HOURS EARLIER —
"Welcome to Grapeside Guesthouse Writers' Retreat," I said, shivering in the chill off the patio doors. I should have taken up station by the gas fireplace, but two men were hogging the warmth. "I'm Elaine, your accommodations coordinator, and that's my husband, Steve, by the bookshelves, pouring wine. We live upstairs, so we're always handy if you need anything. This will be your meeting room all weekend. Coffee, tea and snacks will be available all day. Bathroom in that back corner, behind the long mirror that's right now reflecting our glorious sunset." I waved a hand behind me at the frosted hillsides across the lake, now glowing gold-and-lavender like the backdrop to some mythic play.

"Yeah, hi." Charles, the celebrity author, turned his tweed-clad back. "Hurry, people. I'm starting as soon as everyone's settled."

"Tonight?" a curvy blonde whined, laying a hand on his arm. "But, Charlie . . . ."

"Not now, Angie." He led her toward the wine.

While the writers loaded up their cocktail napkins with local charcuterie, I scanned my emailed list of attendees. Time to put faces to names. One of the two middle-aged women sharing a loveseat waved me over.

"I'm Clare. We've been emailing?"

"Yes, great to meet you at last. Everything's arranged as agreed." I handed Clare (messy ashen bob) and Leigh (faded blond curls) their orientation folders and indicated their cabin on the sketch-map, with its marked path leading slightly downhill from our terrace.

While Leigh glared across at curvy Angie — or maybe at Charles, since there was no visible air between them — Clare pointed to my map. "What's this square thing?"

"The hot tub is off the end of this main building, about halfway up the slope between your cabin and the men's. You'll find thick bathrobes in your guestrooms to make the short walk bearable." Leigh got up abruptly and, giving Angie-Charles a wide berth, tackled the refreshment table. "Um, she doesn't seem thrilled to be here?"

Clare sighed. "I wish she wasn't. But she won the weekend pass and refused to turn down free gourmet food after eating macaroni for months."

They'd raffled off a place at the retreat? News to me. I could only hope Shawna, the caterer and Clare's co-organizer, would prove worthy of Leigh's refined palate.

Angie next. She was the youngest woman by twenty years, the right age for a Hermia or Helena. As I showed her the path to the women's cabin, her wide gaze stayed on Charles's face while he described his suite upstairs, on the same floor as our living quarters. Moving on, I muttered to Steve that Angie was likely to be in Charles' suite come breakfast.

"Bottom to her Titania," Steve murmured, bluntly typecasting Charles as an ass. "Now that everyone's got a drink, I'll go up and see how the meal's coming along."

He slipped out. I and my folders headed for the two men bracketing the fireplace. Both were tall and sandy-haired, but Darren was younger, around Angie's age. Where Barry's winter-white face had ill-tempered creases around eyes and mouth, Darren's laugh lines were stark against his sporty tan. Steve might cast them as Demetrius and Lysander but Barry was too old for either lovesick swain. Three women, two men, and Charles. We were lacking a married couple.

Leigh hurried to the patio door, tapping on the glass. "In here!"

I checked my list. "Celine and Tim?"

"Yes," said Leigh. "My brother and his wife."

Steve would have assigned them roles in 'Dream.' I only let them in and took their coats. The pair hugged Leigh and thanked me for their room assignment: the other suite on this floor, next door to the meeting room. I showed them the hot tub, barely ten paces from their door.

As they helped themselves to wine, I clapped my hands for attention. "Some housekeeping notes: The hot tub is available all night. Just close the cover when you leave, to keep the heat in. Its main lights go off at 11 p.m., but the holiday lights stay on throughout. Supper tonight starts at 6:30, in here. Breakfast in your suites. Lunch will be here, and for supper tomorrow evening you're booked into the Feisty Fig winery down the road. Transportation will be provided. Please ask us for anything you need."

Steve's footsteps descended the foyer stairs in a rush. I hurried out to meet him. "What's wrong?"

"Shawna."

Catering disaster? No! I wasn't competent to cook gourmet suppers. I'd barely learned enough about breakfast to make it through the summer season.

"You keep that wine flowing." Dashing up to my kitchen, I found Shawna darting between stove and island, speedily shifting pots and dishes I didn't recognize. She wore her usual cook's hat but the paper mask over her mouth was new. "Are you sick?"

"My helper's got a bug and I don't want to spread it accidentally. He's out for tonight though. Can you do the remaining salads? Copy the first one." She pointed to seven white square plates and one vegetative sculpture rising from a bed of sprouts.

I washed my hands and began arranging weedy sprouts, translucent celery and paper-thin cucumber rolls. "Not much green here."

She tapped a list taped to the range hood. "One guest avoids green veg for medical reasons. Skip the hot-pressed kale curls on one plate. Tomorrow's lunch buffet will have enough green for the rabbit people."

"Sounds good. You saw the vegetarian, and a gluten-free too?"

"Got 'em covered. It took some adjusting from the meal in the book." She nudged a second page with her spoon handle. It was the same menu I'd pinned up in the guest foyer earlier: gingery squash soup, salad with warm citrus dressing, then crushed-cranberry palate-cleansers gelled into festive shapes, followed by curried entrées, both vegetarian and chicken. Seasonal desserts fit for Falstaff.

"There's a meal this luscious in the book?"

She glanced up. "You didn't read Charles' one and only novel?"

"I skimmed a dismal short story instead," I confessed. "The book's better?"

"It won an award for — and I quote — a tender portrayal of women's complex passions as expressed through food." Her lip curled. "White male achievement: one decent book bought him two decades of writer-in-residence gigs and speaking engagements. Women writers work four times as hard for half the recognition."

"Is that why you and Clare are organizing retreats instead of starring at them? How'd you guys come up with the idea?"

Shawna dumped spices into a mortar and started grinding. "We used to be in the same writers' group back when I was first planning my cookbook and stayed online friends after I quit. When she said the group wanted a retreat, I figured both your business and mine could use the midwinter boost. She did the rest. Although their first pick for guest author fell through, and they ended up with Charles."

"It must be hard to find authors willing to take a last-minute gig a week before Christmas." I speared a sliver of carrot into the first sculpture. "That Angie's always hanging off him. Do authors have groupies?"

Shawna spread the spices on a pan and slid it into the warm oven. "It's the writers' version of a casting couch. Charles wallows in it. After years of supporting his hound-dogging, his wife finally lost patience and bailed. She'd probably poison him if she could, so it's good you vetoed that potluck supper they first proposed."

"Too messy." I spiked more carrot slivers. "Wait. His wife's here?"

"Ex," said Shawna. "Leigh. At least I think they're divorced now, although Clare says there's still some money to settle. I hope they cease fire long enough to give us good reviews. Writer weekends could carry both our businesses through the winter."

Not if this one ended in a flaming scene between Charles and Leigh. No Oberon and Titania, those two. He was an ass and she, well, faded into the background like most grown women in Shakespeare. I reminded myself that women weren't allowed to be actors in his day, which explained why fewer parts were written for them.

"I hope they all buy copies of your cookbook, at least. Did you want to set up a display downstairs?"

"I forgot the box," said Shawna. "I'll bring it tomorrow."

"I'm amazed you can keep all this food organized. You must have a ton of Christmas parties to feed, too."

"Last one's tomorrow night. Ergo the winery reservation for the writers." Shawna scraped the warm spices into a pot and stirred them into the sauce. "Anyway, most of these people joined since I left the group, but I've seen their posts on Clare's Facebook page occasionally. And she's let slip some of the gossip. Angie's into erotic poetry. She's Darren's ex. He writes what he calls cowboy flash. They both met Charles at a writing conference and from what Clare says, Angie was in his bed by the second night. If you see Darren glaring at Charles, that's why."

So Darren was a Lysander after all, and Angie was his low-rent Hermia? Complicated. "Leigh's brother and his wife . . . why sign up for their ex-brother-in-law's retreat?"

"As moral support for Leigh?" Shawna shrugged. "You wouldn't catch me at a retreat led by my ex. But it wasn't supposed to be Charles leading, remember."

"Clare said Leigh's here for the food, and I'm sure she won't be disappointed with all this. What about that other man?"

"Barry? He's been polishing the same novel forever." Shawna gave a strainer full of red grapefruit chunks a shake. "He lost a pre-published writer prize the year Charles was on the awards jury. There were heated words and possibly a revenge shag with Leigh. Clare thinks Barry hopes Charles will be dazzled by his rewrite and finally introduce him to his agent."

Leigh and Charles might be bickering exes but even Steve wouldn't cast them as Oberon and Titania, rulers of the fairies in 'Dream.' We might want to hide the knives, though, in case Leigh decided to audition for Lady Macbeth. "Anything else to do for the salad?"

Shawna handed me a small pitcher. "Now the dressing. Measure a half-cup of that orange-infused oil, mix two tablespoons of coconut balsamic and one of mango honey. Whisk in the grapefruit juice and add the chunks. Stand the jug in hot water so the flavours can meld. So sorry about being short-staffed."

"These things happen." I turned as a door opened nearby. Steve was ushering Charles into his suite across the hall. Had the writer lost his way already? The house wasn't that hard to navigate: only two floors stacked up the hillside, with our living quarters plus the one suite up here, and the other suite plus meeting room — normally the guests' common room — in the walk-out basement.

With the opening reception over, I headed down to clean up. Steve soon followed with cutlery, candlesticks and dishes. As we smoothed cloths over the long table, he said, "Bottom, the ass, travels with a whole pharmacy, from heart pills to the blue ones for bedroom athletics. Angie may be no Titania but she deserves better."

I reached for the wine glasses. "Wait'll you hear about the rest of the cast."

The room's conversion to a candlelit dining hall was complete by the time the writers reassembled. We left them with pre-dinner drinks and hurried up to help Shawna. While she concentrated like a mad chemist, adding single drops of grapeseed extract and other healthy oils to the salads, Steve carried down a platter of cold appies. I followed with mini-meatball skewers and braised bison cubes.

Two steps into the room Charles all but wiped me out with an elbow as he pontificated about a book tour. I dodged, barely saving the tray.

Tim called out, "Who did you sucker into paying for that trip, Charles?"

Charles turned beet-red. He snatched up three garlicky meatballs skewers and sucked them into his maw. Leigh shook a finger at him. "Cholesterol."

With a slit-eyed glare, Charles grabbed more skewers, rolling them in the garlic mustard for good measure. Gross. This was the man who wrote seductively about food?

Once the guests found seats, we served the soup, filling the air with spicy aromas. Next, I ladled the warm dressing onto the salad sculptures. Steve took the first tray down, quoting something about a 'sallet to cool a man's stomach.'

"The one with no kale is for Charles," Shawna told me. "And

Barry's the vegetarian so make sure he gets the disguised tofurkey instead of the real butter chicken." I served those and brought the last sticky soup plates upstairs. Steve was gloomily surveying the contents of our fridge.

"Sorry," I said. "I was too busy to make supper."

Shawna pointed to my kitchen table, where she'd set out two bowls. "Dive in."

The soup was every bit as good as it smelled. With our tummies pleasantly warmed, we hefted the crushed-cranberry palate cleansers on their chilled trays. The festive gelatin molds glowed on tiny white plates. The guests' cheer quotient rose as they identified bells, Christmas trees and a Santa. All was calm, all was bright until, somehow, half of Clare's red holly-leaf jumped from her spoon into Angie's copious cleavage. Giggling, Angie fished it out, flashing a lot of boob in the process. Tim gaped. Celine elbowed him, with a sideways glance at Angie so coldly calculating that Lady Macbeth might recoil from it.

Barry said, "Almost like that incident in your book, Charles. You know, the first flickerings of sensual tension. Not that Clare wants Angie."

Clare's lip curled with a disdain that revealed her potential for queenly roles. "You're not wrong about that."

So much for that first hint of seasonal cheer.

Ten minutes later we lugged the savory entrées down, making sure Barry got the vegetarian one. Then we sat upstairs, gobbling spare butter chicken while Shawna set up dessert: poinsettia-themed stands with warm, cinnamon-y, mince tartlets, cranberry nut squares, bite-sized rounds of rich chocolate ganache and other incredible edibles. Steve and I carried them down. Shawna brought the hot-drink carafes but stayed out in the foyer, stacking dirty dishes onto trays as we brought them out.

While I cleared his entrée plate, Barry said, "You really don't recognize this meal, Charles? Page 70?"

"My book wasn't set at Christmas." Charles lurched upright,

crumbs down his shirt and a syrupy currant stuck to his moustache. Definitely Falstaff. He belched. "Like you all, I too was once a humble, hopeful amateur. That was before I won the esteemed Gallworthy Prize, of course." He went on but I didn't stay to hear. Slogging dirty dishes upstairs and helping Shawna clean her pots were chores even Steve preferred over listening to Charles make an ass of himself.

"I hope the online reviews won't penalize us for Charles," I told Shawna. "Was their first-choice writer less egotistical?"

"Much." Shawna packed her pots and utensils in some complex pattern I didn't try to follow. "Lids now please."

I handed them over. "Why'd that one cancel?"

"Stomach bug. Very last-minute."

The writers eventually called it a night. We cleared up the common room, nibbling leftover desserts as we went. First day done. As we crawled into bed, Steve said, "The more Charles drank, the more he boasted."

"He seemed pretty well pickled." I yawned. "No wonder Angie went back to her own room."

"For it will come to pass that every braggart shall be found an ass," he said, and turned off the light.

I woke later with indigestion. Beyond my bedroom window, sloshing sounds and whimpers told me the hot tub was occupied. When I got back into bed, I had to pull the pillow over my head as the unmistakable sex noises escalated.

Steve groaned in the darkness. "Little blue pills for the win."

And here I thought he'd go for something about the revels being ended, or Puck's goodnight speech at the end of 'Dream.' "Better check the water level in the morning," I muttered. "They're making some serious waves out there."

Morning came too early. We served Charles a breakfast for two. Angie wasn't there but he scarfed most of it anyway. For the writers' coffee break, we refilled beverages and set out Shawna's hot, fresh muffins. Back to work they all went while Shawna prepped lunch: another fabulous soup, green salad and fresh buns, beef rolls filled with cinnamon-scented mincemeat, sliced turkey with cranberry chutney and what Shawna called a bison terrine—spicy ground meat baked in a flaky pastry case. When I asked about the intense flavours she showed us the secret: cassia cinnamon imported from China.

That afternoon, Charles took the writers individually to his suite for manuscript consultations. Nobody stayed more than a quarter hour and Leigh didn't go at all. Barry had barely closed the door before we heard shouting. There was a wall-shaking thud. He barreled out of the suite and straight outside to stomp off along the hillside.

"If they broke anything, I'm charging it to Charles," I muttered to Steve.

"Shh!"

Charles stood in the suite's doorway, rubbing one wrist. He yelled, "Next" down the stairs. Angie came up with her sweater pulled so low I could almost see her belly button. Soon we heard her giggling. I rolled my eyes and turned on the radio to cover the noise. How many blue pills could Charles handle before he overdosed?

Two hours later, the winery van was at the door. Barry came back and scrambled into his seat without speaking to anyone. The rest gradually arrived from their cabins. Angie and Charles reappeared together and joined the others in the van.

"Did you see his neck?" Steve murmured. "How blunter than a serpent's tooth is Angie's love bite."

I shrugged. She'd distracted Charles when it mattered.

Hopefully they'd get through supper with civility. We didn't need our guests making trouble at neighbouring businesses.

After we readied the common room for the next day, we treated ourselves to leftovers and crawled into bed, hoping Charles and Angie had worked out their hot tub fantasies last night. A good night's sleep—was that too much to ask?

Sometime later, a door slammed against a wall. I sat abruptly upright and reached the kitchen in time to see Tim shove a protesting Charles toward his suite. Charles wrenched away, staggered and would have gone headlong down the stairs if Tim hadn't grabbed him. As I flipped on the kitchen light, Tim looked over his shoulder.

"Sorry about the noise."

"Need help?"

"I've got it, thanks."

I returned to bed, drawing my curtains tighter against the festive lights around the deserted hot tub.

Half an hour later I was up again, hunting for another banging door while chill breezes twined around my ankles. Once more it was the door to Charles' suite, but the cold air poured through his open balcony door. I called his name. No answer came from the mounded duvet. He must have woken from his drunken haze longing for fresh air and then crawled back into bed. I crept across the dark room, closed the balcony door, and made my way out again. Please, no more banging tonight. Of any variety.

There was none. No noise at all for long enough to thoroughly submerge me in well-earned slumber.

Until the screaming started, right beneath my bedroom window.

Angie's screams brought everyone from all three buildings, and only stopped when Darren hauled her back to our terrace. The others followed in twos and threes. By then I'd checked for a pulse and Steve had called 911. Which brought me back to the unpleasant present moment: standing by the hot tub, alone on the moon-frosted hillside, while the police tried to get their car unstuck and Steve ministered to our surviving guests. Rather than freeze in the breeze for the next half hour, I trudged back to the common room and counted noses through the patio doors.

Tim and Celine huddled on the nearest bench, she in a flannel nightie and he in a faded sweatshirt over his dress pants. Their booted feet sat amid the loose gravel and wet shoes left by the others. Darren and Barry were further in, two manly solitudes staring stoically at the opposite wall. Barry was dressed as he had been for supper, but with green plaid slippers now damp from snow-melt. Darren wore sweatpants and bare feet, his bare chest showing beneath his jacket. Leigh and Clare clung to each other at the table. A flash of silver glimmered in Clare's hair. Leigh brushed that away.

Angie?

The bathroom door opened. Accounted for, in the baggy sleep pants and hoodie she'd been wearing by the hot tub.

I stepped indoors to be greeted with a clamour of voices.

"Who is it?"

"Is it Charles?"

"Oh, poor Charlie!"

"Was it his heart?" asked Leigh.

Steve gave a minute shake of his head, a warning I didn't need. It wasn't our place to spell out brutal murder.

"It's Charles," I said. "The police and coroner will determine cause of death."

Silence fell. I looked at all the faces around the room,

wondering who was strong enough, angry enough, to beat Charles and manhandle him into our hot tub. Leigh? Motive enough but a lot smaller than her ex. Tim? Burly enough but he'd helped Charles earlier. Barry had the fight; there might be wiry muscle in his skinny arms. Darren lost his girlfriend, making him both strong and motivated. Her head lay on his shoulder now. And — I took a closer look to be sure — the hems of her Tweetie-Bird sleep pants were damp. Was it from dragging them over the frosty path or from splashes when she tipped Charles headfirst into the tub?

There were as many motives here as people, but those didn't answer the who, the how or, most significantly, the when. Between the drunken stumbling, doors banging and then the icy drafts, it's not like we were sound asleep all night. We should have heard the beating. Beside me, Steve eyed everyone too. Who was he casting as First Murderer, Second Murderer and so on? We couldn't exactly exchange notes in front of the surviving guests. But if this wasn't cleared up quickly, we'd be dumping our dream retirement at a steep discount to huddle in some tiny apartment with no view at all, getting on each other's nerves over endless games of Scrabble.

Well, I wasn't giving up without a fight. I might not be able to make the murderer expose himself as Hamlet tried with his nefarious uncle, but if I played my lines right, I could start the suspects bickering amongst themselves and revealing clues. I stood up.

"Ahem. While we're waiting for the police, let's get a few things out in the open."

Everyone but Angie looked up.

"Half of you hated Charles," said Steve, picking up his cue like a pro. "Never a borrower nor a lender be, but Tim made snide comments about Charles and money. Did he owe you, Tim?"

Tim lurched to his feet. Celine hauled him down. "Shut up."

"Too late for that," I said. "If you don't tell us, the police can find out."

Under our combined stares, Tim confessed. But not to murder. Five years ago, Charles had convinced him to invest in a summer school for writers, renting a whole mountain resort for a month. But only five people paid a deposit, and three of those withdrew when the balance came due. Charles hadn't bothered with cancellation insurance and the resort claimed the balance. Instead of making huge profits, Tim was out a good chunk of his life savings. That could turn any man to the role of First Murderer.

"Of course he was angry," Celine said. "I was, too, and I'm not sorry Charles is dead. But killing him wouldn't get our money back." Her mouth twisted. "I'm not the only one glad he's dead. I'm not the one who got in a fist-fight with him this afternoon." She glared at Barry. "Come on. We all heard your 'feedback session'."

"He told me I was still a hack," Barry said in a flat voice. "I told him he should talk, since he wasn't even a real author. I said . . . well, I said if he didn't give my manuscript to his agent, I'd reveal that he'd plagiarized his book. He tried to pop me one and I grabbed his arm. It was over in half a minute."

"Hardly the slaying of Mercutio," Steve observed. "But you're still dressed in your clothes from supper. Where were you after the winery van brought everyone back?"

"I went for another walk."

Steve peered over his glasses. "In the dark?"

"I knew the route from this afternoon, and the moon was up. I got back maybe a half hour before the screaming started."

"When you came back, you saw nothing, nobody, around the hot tub?" I asked. "Were the lights on or off?"

Barry scratched his stubbly chin. "Seems to me the big lights went off as I came back. I didn't see anyone." His eyes flicked across the room. "Or not tonight, anyway. Darren, now . . . he wanted Angie back. Looks like he finally got her."

Angie sat up. "Don't you make insinuations! Poor Charlie's not even cold."

Barry's lip curled. "You were only with poor Charlie in hopes of getting his agent to look at your work. Think I didn't see you riding Cowboy D Friday night in the hot tub? My bedroom looks right down there, and my eyes weren't dazzled by the big lights then."

Whoa! Angie had been hooking up with Darren? Good thing this wasn't a Shakespeare play. Old Willie had a rough way with faithless women.

"A besotted Helena to his Lysander," Steve murmured to me while Angie called Barry a voyeur and several less polite names. I chewed my lip. If Angie and Darren were making waves the first night, had they also collaborated tonight, like Lady Macbeth and her ambitious lord? It was hard to see why they'd kill Charles, but there had been a fair bit of blood seeping around the older man's head. Gosh. Would we have to call in professional crime-scene cleaners for the hot tub?

Barry called Angie a slut. Angie burst into tears. Darren tried to punch Barry. Tim shoved Darren into a chair. "Stay," he growled, rather like the lion in Midsummer Night's Dream.

Steve handed Angie a tissue with an avuncular air I recognized from when he played Leonato in 'Much Ado.' What he said, though, came from Henry IV. "Now, child, redeem your banished honours." At her blank stare, he added, "I mean, tell me all, to repair your slandered reputation."

Angie confessed she'd never stopped seeing Darren. "Charlie wasn't any good in bed," she sniffed, gazing up at Steve as if that was explanation enough. She'd realized early on that Charles would never recommend her or Darren to his agent, and had strung him along anyway, hoping to meet the agent herself. "I didn't kill him, though. Me and Darren, we were, well . . . since Barry wasn't around at their place . . . ."

Darren shook his head frantically. Angie didn't notice, but Leigh did. She laughed, as filled with spite as King Lear's evil daughter Regan.

"Charles caught you together, didn't he? I told him you'd be at it like bunnies again if he pretended to be pissed. He'd have blacklisted you with every agent and publisher in the country."

Celine took up the evil-daughter role. "Did he burst in on you? Did hot-head Darren charge at him? Kicks to the ribs, a bit of internal bleeding?"

"How'd you know about his ribs?" I tried to ask Celine, but by then everyone was yelling.

A headlight glanced off the patio door from the driveway below. Steve murmured, "I shall away to light the paths for those rude mechanicals." Ignoring my glare, he plodded away like a middle-aged and balding Puck.

The yelling gradually died into a lot of sulky side-eye. Tim slunk back to his wife and Angie stood behind Darren, rubbing his shoulders. I was trying to think of other questions when Steve passed the patio doors with two uniformed officers. He came back alone and beckoned me into a huddle by the patio doors. If he opened with yet another Shakespeare quote, I'd be tempted to smack him.

He didn't. "They found drag marks from the men's cabin down to the hot tub. They're searching up there for signs of struggle."

Aha! Real evidence at last. I gazed severely at Darren, and then at Barry. "The police are searching your rooms. Is there anything you'd like to tell us?"

Barry stared back, unabashed. Having confessed his attempt at blackmailing Charles, he had apparently nothing else on his conscience.

Darren drooped. "My room. There was a bit of struggle when Charles barged in."

"Go on." Steve gestured, imperious as Oberon.

Darren spread out his hands. "I swear I didn't touch him. I was kinda tangled in the sheets. Angie jumped like a . . . well, she got up first."

"Charlie grabbed my arm," Angie said indignantly. She leaned against Darren's shoulder and picked a piece of white gravel out of her sock. "I pushed him off and he kind of wobbled. He didn't hit his head or anything, just . . . sat down. We thought he passed out. I hoped if he woke up somewhere else he'd forget being there at all. I didn't know he had a bad heart."

Steve looked at her sadly. "How sharper than a serpent's tooth."

Ignoring him, I snapped my fingers for Angie's attention. "You both dragged him down to the hot tub. Did you go straight back to your interrupted activities?"

"No," cried Angie. "I went back to my room. Darren? Did you hurt him?"

Darren didn't look nearly as offended as I expected him to. "Charles was breathing okay, honest. We leaned him against the tub, so he'd stay warm. I was straightening up my room when Barry came back."

Barry nodded. "His light was on and I heard him moving around."

I spun toward the table. "Clare? Leigh? Can either of you recall Angie's return?"

Clare raised her hand. "I heard her door slam. Didn't hear her leave again though, not until she screamed."

Steve shook his head at me, "Even a serpent's tooth would need some upper body strength to string up the dead weight of Charles." He eyed Leigh sternly. "You wanted your pound of flesh. You set Charles up. Did you hope he'd have a heart attack over Angie's betrayal?"

Leigh sneered. "Why would I know about his bad heart? We haven't lived together in years."

"Cholesterol," I blurted out. "You warned him about it when he took more meatballs last night."

"So you did know?" Steve pointed a finger at her. "Did you find him passed out and helpless, and get in a few kicks while he was down? Who helped you tip him over the tub? Was it your devoted brother?"

Clare hugged her friend protectively. "It was me who found him, not her. When she told me how she'd set him up to catch Angie, I went to break it up before there was a brawl. As the retreat's organizer I'd feel responsible if they damaged the cabin. But I fell over Charles's legs. He snored like any drunk then." She bit her lip. "I tied his wrists and legs in tinsel, so he'd have to call for help to get free. He was a womanizing ass, and he deserved to be humiliated."

"She wasn't gone more than ten minutes," said Leigh. "After she came back and told me, I sat in my room with the window open, waiting for him to wake up. You can't see the hot tub from there, but I wanted to enjoy his begging for help until everyone woke up and saw."

"From that cold heart let Heaven engender hail," Steve quoted, from Antony and Cleopatra. Leigh was no Queen of Egypt, though. More like the asp.

"And you just sat waiting?" I asked her. "Wasn't he stalling you over money?"

"That's wrong," Clare snapped. "He wanted spousal support from her because he wasn't earning anything. That's why I asked him to step in for the retreat, so he'd have to show some income. She's better off with —"

"With him dead," I finished. But Leigh couldn't have lifted him alone. She'd need help from Clare, or faithful Polonius, er, Tim. "Tim and Celine: both Angie and Clare had to walk right past your suite, and your bedroom window faces that way. Did you see or hear either of them?"

"No," said Celine. She had a firm grip on Tim's arm, but he shook her off.

"I saw Charles out the window. My sister never went past. I'll swear to that."

"Sure you will." Steve leaned over him, looking more like a Midsomer Murders interrogator than anyone I could think of from Shakespeare. "You were the closest to the scene, and you had thousands of reasons to hate Charles."

Something had been niggling at me. "Angie, where'd that gravel come from in your sock? You weren't out there without boots on, were you?"

"Nope." She looked around vaguely, and then pointed behind Darren's chair. "Right there." I looked. Just like the floor near the doorway, there were damp smears and white gravel.

"Right where you were standing earlier, Tim. If you never went out there, where'd you get the gravel?"

Too late I realized that proved nothing. Everybody had gone up or down that path since Angie screamed. And Tim's boots had been planted in that wet, gravelly patch beside the bench until Darren's outburst.

Fortunately, Tim wasn't any faster on the uptake. "Yeah, okay," he muttered grumpily. "I thought Charles might get hypothermia if he stayed out all night, so I went out to help him back to bed."

"And failed to move him," said Steve. "Why?"

"I couldn't see his breath. I tried for a pulse, but my hands were too cold to feel one. I figured since Leigh's a nurse's aide, she'd know what to do. So, I called her."

Leigh shrugged off Clare's protective arms. "I was sure it was his heart. Charles is usually careful with his medications, but with all the drinking he might've forgotten to take them. Alcohol and blood thinners shouldn't mix anyway. So, I crushed up an aspirin and ran up to the tub to put it under his tongue."

Tim slumped. "By the time she got there he'd stopped breathing completely. I'd cut most of the tinsel, so we laid him down to try chest compressions. When bruises showed up on his ribs we were terrified we'd be blamed for him dying. Leigh might lose her job. She's got hardly any pension. So . . . ."

Celine said, "I suggested we make it look accidental. Like he was stumbling around in the dark, bumping into things, tripping over trailing Christmas decorations. He wouldn't be the first drunk to drown in a hot tub." She shrugged, cool as the frosty hillside. "Once his head was in the tub, I wound the light string around his leg. Simple."

Staged, as I'd thought from the first. And Celine had choreographed it. But we couldn't prove Charles was alive when he went into the water, so we couldn't prove he was killed. At best, the whole bunch could be found guilty of indignity to a dead body.

As I watched the guests' sad, mad, scared faces, I realized there was another possibility. If Charles had, say, doubled up his blood-thinning medication during his Friday night binge, he'd bruise easily on Saturday from Barry's grab and Angie's love-bites. Walking over to the men's cabin would have drained the blood from his brain, causing his eventual faint. Darren and Angie didn't want to be blacklisted in the publishing industry — not that I thought anyone there would care if two nobodies had sex — so they dragged Charles away, probably bruising him more in the process. Clare, finding him passed out, had likely bruised him further while tying him in tinsel. Unbeknownst to any of them, he'd been slowly bleeding out internally because of the excess blood-thinners. The blood in the hot tub would have seeped through the tissues in his mouth and nose. I'd assessed a few similarly over-medicated seniors in ER.

A tidal wave of relief sent me staggering to a chair. It wasn't our fault. A guest had died accidentally due to his own medication error.

An RCMP officer leaned in the patio door. "Can anyone here identify the body?"

Leigh put up her hand. "He's my ex-husband. We think he messed up his blood thinner medication while drunk. You'll find the prescription in his room."

"I can take you up," said Steve. A different constable followed him through to the stairs. The first cop took Leigh outside. I watched them talking through the glass doors, breath steaming in the cold night. For just a moment I had a vertiginous flashback to Charles steaming in my hot tub. No wonder Angie had screamed when she saw him.

I frowned. "Angie, why did you go back out?" She slitted her eyes at Darren, which was as good as a confession in the circumstances. My brain sparked another flashback. "Barry, what did you mean about Charles plagiarizing his book?"

Barry blinked. "It was the food. All those dishes, some slightly altered for Christmas, were in his famous book and he didn't even recognize them. I thought back to our early writing group, how surprised we all were that a guy who'd only ever shown us lame noir knock-offs could have this sensual, literary feast inside him. Then I remembered that cooking student."

Clare opened her mouth, but Celine got in first. "The poetic one? That girl Charles moved on at her very first meeting?" She glanced at Leigh. "Sorry, dear, but you know how he was with the young ones."

"He probably offered to read her work and told her she was no good." Barry's fists clenched. "And then got an agent by pretending it was his. I can't believe I wasted twenty years trying to impress a damned plagiarizing hack."

Leigh dropped her head into her hands. "When she quit coming to meetings, I just thought she got bored with trying to be a writer. How did you know, Barry?"

"I watched him gobble up that food without even noticing the similarities." He rubbed his wrist. "When I accused him yesterday, he attacked me."

"A cooking student, you said?" I fetched the menu from the foyer. Now that I knew what I was looking for — foods that were contra-indicated if you were taking blood-thinners — there they all were. "Grapefruit and juice, grapeseed extract, cranberries, lashings of garlic, ginger, turmeric. All blood thinning foods. Cinnamon everywhere."

"Look to the baked meats." Steve's thumbs tapped over his phone screen. "That special cinnamon . . . cassia cinnamon has twice as much blood thinner as regular cinnamon. How much of it did Charles eat?"

I mentally tallied the suspect foods. "He might as well have tripled his blood-thinner dose in his few meals. That menu was no accident. And Leigh was conveniently here to play Chief Suspect if anyone got suspicious. Clare, what happened to the first author you booked?"

She swallowed. "Food poisoning after a book launch in Kelowna last week."

"Catered, right? And how did you pick a winner for the retreat pass?"

Clare's face paled. "I didn't. Shawna did. She's . . . that student . . . ."

Headlights came up the drive. A cop opened the door. "Expecting someone?"

Steve and I both looked at the clock. 5 a.m. already. "I do hear the morning lark," he said sadly.

"It's Shawna, the caterer," I told the cop with a heavy heart. "Here to start brunch prep. I think you'll really want to talk to her."

PICKLED TO DEATH
BY CHARLOTTE MORGANTI

Persimmon B. Worthing
  6547 Gardenia Lane
Blossom City, B.C.

October 30, 2019

Dear Violet,
   At last, a letter from your favourite aunt! I apologize for my lengthy silence, however I *do* have an excellent excuse.
   You know our town council prides itself on Blossom City's peaceful, laid-back personality, but when I reflect on the last few weeks I'm convinced that sentiment is merely a delusional wish. Life in our small Okanagan town lately has left me little time to take a deep breath. That, my dear niece, is my long-winded way of saying I couldn't write sooner because I've been a tad occupied helping Sergeant Courgette.
   There's no reason to tell your mother what I've been up to, Violet. She will feel obligated to chastise me about what she

calls my need to meddle, and from there things will go rapidly downhill. She can't accept that I see the nudges and hints I give Courgette as performing my civic duty — he is a relative newcomer to town (arriving not long before you were born, in fact). Since he isn't privy to the intricate inter-relationships and history of Blossom City locals, he often misses vital clues. As someone who loves her town and most of the people in it, I must do my utmost to help Courgette protect us.

Enough self-justification. I won't keep you in suspense any longer.

Here's the latest:

For the first time ever, Blossom City's renowned Perfect Pickle Competition ended without a winner. Can you believe that? It's rocked the town to its soul.

More unsettling than a failure to crown a champion pickler is that the whole affair nearly pickled my dear friend Lacey Lavender's patootie. At the risk of putting too boastful a spin on it, had I not shared a few observations with Sergeant Courgette, Lacey would still be sporting an ankle bracelet and getting crocked on vodka tonics behind my garden gate while she awaited trial for murder.

Yes, murder!

This year's Perfect Pickle Competition initially followed all the traditions we townspeople love. As usual, the competition took place on a September Saturday under the cover of a large tent in our fairgrounds. The hopeful entrants were members of Blossom City's three pickle clubs: The Dillers, Les Moutardes and The Unbeetables; Herb Marvel, our local doctor who is blessed with a voice that gives me the most delicious shivers, acted as emcee; and Daisy Johnston was the sole judge. Even Daisy adhered to tradition — her L'Air du Temps perfume announced her arrival some thirty seconds before she swept into the tent, trailing her trademark gauzy (and I must say, ever so slightly gaudy) floor-length duster behind her.

"Fellow lovers of brined vegetables," Dr. Marvel said, "please welcome our judge, a woman who possesses more Pickle Jar trophies than I've delivered babies. Daiseeeee Johnston!" As the crowd applauded, Daisy advanced to centre-tent and studied the rows of oilcloth-covered tables, bearing jars of pickles, that lined the tent's perimeter. "My, my, what an alluring array of pickles."

She assessed the contestants standing behind their entries and gave us a crooked-toothed smile. "And what a lovely group of picklers."

As she spoke her opening two lines, several people mouthed the words along with her. Tradition.

Daisy pointed at the Dillers' banner. "This year, let's start with the dills, shall we?"

Lacey nudged me as we stood behind our pickled candy-stripe beets. "The Dillers. What a surprise. As if we don't remember where she starts every year."

I nodded and yawned. I recognized every member of the Dillers, down-to-earth lovers of the humble pickling cucumber. Frankly, I find them boring. Not the Dillers, but the cucumbers. Whether it's an heirloom or an organic, what is a cucumber but a green vegetable? And the transformation that colour undergoes when it hits the brine? Most unfortunate.

As Daisy approached, the Dillers straightened their posture, smoothed their clothing and sipped from water bottles. Before she accepted the first toothpick-speared dill from a contestant, Daisy turned in a slow circle, surveying the tent. "Rosette?" Her voice bounced off the canvas overhead. "Where are you? I must cleanse my palate."

Rosette Adams jogged into the tent, a lithe, vibrant vision in red, from the glossy curls piled haphazardly atop her head to her barely-out-of-the-box sneakers. She carried a mid-sized wicker basket filled with water bottles, paper cocktail napkins, small green leaves and packages of crackers.

"Whoa," Lacey whispered. "Rosette returns."

"And she's a redhead now," I said.

Daisy smiled at the crowd. "Rosette has graciously agreed to assist me today."

The crowd applauded.

Daisy snapped her fingers. "Cracker. Water."

Rosette sprang forward, her flame-coloured updo swaying. She passed Daisy a bottle of Blossom City Sparkling Water. Small green leaves floated in the liquid. Daisy selected a cracker, chomped and took a healthy slug of water.

"Excellent," she said. "Minted water. The best palate cleanser available." She tossed the bottle's cap into Rosette's basket, grasped the open bottle and reached for the first of many dills on toothpicks.

I asked Lacey, "Do you think Daisy's paying Rosette?" Rosette had fallen on hard times ever since the Perfect Pickle Competition two years ago when she was disqualified for cheating.

"I hope so," Lacey said. "I never expected Les Moutardes to eject their founder from the club. And who'd have thought her online pickle business would crater?"

"It's not your fault," I said. "You saw a wrong and reported it. Anyone would."

Daisy and Rosette had made their way to the last of the Dillers. Daisy ate a cracker, swigged her minted water and swallowed. She dabbed her lips with the napkin Rosette handed her, then popped the last slice of dill into her mouth, savoured it and swallowed. She wiped her brow with the back of her hand. "Next year I would love air conditioning in the tent."

Rosette flapped an ornamental fan in front of Daisy's flushed face.

Daisy was correct — the tent was steamier than, well between you and me, Violet, than those bodice-rippers your mother reads. I cracked open a bottle of Blossom City Sparkling Water and sipped.

"Minted water as a palate cleanser," Lacey said. "A little over the top, don't you think?"

I shrugged. "Appearing pretentious is a risk I bet Daisy's willing to take. You don't have a real mojito if you omit the mint."

"Nooo! You think?"

"Oh yes. I saw her mother at the liquor store yesterday. Does that woman have anything in her closet except fleece sweat suits? Anyway, she had white rum in her basket and told me she was running Daisy's errands. 'Mustn't forget the mint and club soda. Daisy so enjoys her mojitos,' she said."

"You're kidding!" Lacey glanced toward the table of Red Regular beet pickles where Tulip Johnston, a white-haired, petite (and of course older) version of Daisy, stood in her turquoise fleece. "Tulip runs her daughter's errands?"

"I was a bit taken aback too. When I asked if shopping tired her, Tulip said, 'Since I moved into Golden Times Homestead, life has been a string of deadly days with nothing to do but stare at the hummingbird feeder outside my window. I'd gladly run the whole town's errands to get out of that sorry excuse for God's waiting room.' I'm guessing Tulip's not a happy homesteader."

Daisy's voice rang out. "Onward, Rosette. Mustard pickles next." She sailed over to Les Moutardes. (If you ever want to learn how to put on airs and graces, Violet, just study Les Moutardes. High falutin' yellow bellies, Lacey and I call them.)

Daisy and Rosette worked their way along the tables. Daisy sampled, swallowed, crunched a cracker and swigged her palate cleanser before moving to the next entry. Every now and then she steadied herself by putting a hand on Rosette's shoulder or leaning against the pickle tables. If I was correct about the contents of her water bottle, the ratio of rum to soda in her mojito must have been off the charts.

Lacey elbowed me. "Ashley's next. Years have passed and she's still furious."

I glanced over at Ashley Jones, until four years ago the frequent co-winner of the award for best mustard pickles. Her winning streak ended when her partner, Basil Phickle, retired from competition and took up with Daisy. (Don't you love the irony that Daisy, who had a nasty allergy to the herb, would date a man named Basil?)

Daisy blotted her skin with a napkin and then accepted a speared cauliflower pickle from Ashley. "Not going to poison me this year, are you dear?"

Ashley sneered. "As I say every year, how I wish I'd thought of that. However, if I were going to poison anyone, *dear,* it would be that louse Basil."

Daisy shrugged and took a tiny bite of the pickle. She grimaced and tossed the remainder onto the tablecloth. "Your product has certainly gone downhill since Basil parted ways with you. We know who had the talent in your former partnership."

Ashley flushed and glared at Daisy, who offered up a cherubic smile.

Finally, again complaining about the heat and urging Rosette to fan her more vigorously, Daisy turned her attention to The Unbeetables, the pickling club Lacey and I belonged to. I peeked at the front of my T-shirt, worried that the sweat running down my breastbone was visible.

The Unbeetables began as a club for beet picklers but over the years devolved into three somewhat friendly factions: Golden Globes, Candystripers and Red Regulars. Every year for the last five years an Unbeetable beet, usually a Red Regular, has won the coveted Pickle Jar trophy for the best all-round pickle.

Lacey vowed this year to snatch the Pickle Jar trophy from the Red Regulars. In my humble opinion, Lacey should have won last year, but Daisy awarded the trophy to her mother, eighty-three-year-old Tulip, declaring that her Red Regular pickle glowed like a prize ruby.

The loss still irks Lacey.

Daisy tasted the four Golden Globe entries, cleansing her palate between every sample as tradition dictated. "Very nice, could be a contender," she said, after each sample.

"She's trying to convince us she isn't biased," Lacey said.

I snorted. "Yeah, just like I believe her mother didn't put food colouring in last year's winning entry." I raised my water bottle to my lips.

My station was the first of the Candystripers, next to the gap between the Golden Globe table and ours. When Daisy approached, I quickly set down my water bottle and speared a particularly gorgeous candy-striped pickle from my jar. Daisy put her drink bottle onto the table, accepted my offering and inspected it. "Exquisite striping, Persimmon." She tasted. "Oh, wonderful flavour, well done."

You'll think me silly to get emotional about a pickled beet but those words immediately went to my head. Or perhaps it was all that standing in a hot tent. When Daisy extended her hand, I couldn't grasp hold. The light in the tent had dimmed; her hand seemed to be there, and not there.

When I next opened my eyes Lacey's face hovered above me and I realized I was sitting on the ground between the tables. My jar of pickles, along with both my and Daisy's water bottles, had tumbled to the grass, their contents seeping out. The aromas of rum and pickle brine wafted upward. Not an appetizing mix.

"You fainted," Daisy said. "Spilled everything."

I looked at the pickles and water bottles beside me. "I'm sorry."

Rosette collected the bottles. "I have extra water for Daisy. No problem."

"Fortunately I tasted your pickles before they hit the ground," Daisy said. "Can Rosette give you a hand up?"

I struggled to my feet, sat in a chair behind our table and waved them away. "Carry on. I'll be fine."

Daisy stood still for a moment, resting her hand on Rosette's shoulder. "Whew, the fright I got when Persimmon fainted has affected me." She shook her head and took deep breaths. "Right, that's better. Onward."

She spied Lacey's pickles. "What have you to offer this year, Lacey?"

She examined Lacey's sample. "Yesssss, marginally better than last year. Which if I'm not mistaken, almost won you the trophy?" She pointed to the rings in the beet. "But you see that bleeding of colour here, and here? That's what tripped you up last year and might do the same this year."

"Really?" Lacey said, her voice dropping the temperature in the tent by ten degrees.

"Of course," Daisy said. "You didn't lose because my mother allegedly added food colouring to her pickles. You didn't lose because I allegedly favoured family. You lost because you cannot perfect the pickling process. Frankly, you should have spent more time this year working on pickling basics instead of snooping around trying to prove my mother cheated or that I'm biased."

She stretched her lips in a tight smile. "That said, I am still willing to judge your efforts, wanting as they may be." She took a bite of Lacey's sample and swallowed. "Needs work," she said. When she tossed the remains of Lacey's sample onto the oilcloth it skittered toward me. I marvelled at the perfect imprint of Daisy's crooked front tooth in the beet.

Daisy moved away. Rosette tucked a few stray locks into her fragile updo and smiled at Lacey. "Better luck next year."

"Right," Lacey said. "The only way I'll have a chance of winning is if she overdoses on pickles and dies."

When Daisy neared the end of the Candystripers pickles, her mother Tulip left her station among the Red Regular picklers and came over, shuffling her sensibly-shod feet along the grass. As she reached me she tripped and jostled our table, rocking the open pickle jars. "Oops," she said, "new shoes, uneven grass. Lacey's pickles almost ended up on the grass alongside yours." She fumbled for the lid, replaced it, and then brushed the table clear of the remnants of the pickle Daisy had tossed onto the oilcloth. "There, that's better. How are you feeling, Persimmon?"

"I'm fine. You best get back. Daisy has almost reached your station."

When Tulip shuffled off, Lacey said, "Things at the home must really be boring. That's the first time she's lifted a finger to help anyone."

Lacey was in a pout so I didn't bother to contradict her. However, Tulip and I belonged to the Garden Club and before she moved into Golden Times Homestead, Tulip and I had often helped tend their gardens.

Back to the events of the day, however. Tulip reached her station with seconds to spare. She speared a pickle from her jar and handed it to her daughter. Daisy put down her water bottle. She swiped at her brow with a cocktail napkin and sucked in a deep breath. She patted her chest, smiled at Tulip, and popped the pickle into her mouth. She chewed, swallowed and fell backward onto the grass, pale and still.

The tent exploded into chaos. Rosette screamed and dropped her basket. Dr. Marvel rushed across the tent and examined Daisy's prone figure. He shouted, "Call 911," and began CPR.

Lacey punched madly at her phone screen, saying, "On it."

Tulip hovered next to Daisy, moaning. Rosette crawled around nearby, alternating between brushing loose strands of red hair away from her face and cramming spilled and wayward items into her basket.

I joined Lacey on the fringes of the crowd. Across the tent Ashley stood by her table looking like someone who'd won Lotto 6/49.

Several minutes later we heard sirens and saw flashing lights. Soon paramedics entered the tent and took over from Dr. Marvel. Close on the heels of the ambulance crew was Sergeant Courgette of the local police. I waved at him and he strode over.

"Bonjour, Persimmon," Courgette said. His "bonjour" bore no hint of either France or Quebec. Despite his French name, he's as Anglo as most of us in Blossom City. Still, he believes Frenchness and a facility for the language is in his blood. I've never had the heart to challenge his misguided belief.

"Hello, Milton," I said.

"Umm." Courgette leaned closer and whispered, "Sergeant Courgette, please."

I raised an eyebrow in question.

He straightened and adjusted his cap. "I am in uniform. Therefore, official. So, Sergeant Courgette." He waved his arm at the scene around us. "Excusez. Duty calls."

As my gaze followed his gesture, I noticed Rosette tidying the tent. She dumped trash into the container near the side exit and then began replacing lids on the mustard pickle jars and brushing debris from the tabletops onto the grass. I was about to tell her to put the debris into a bin when Ashley approached her with a small garbage can and took over.

Suddenly Tulip wailed loudly. Dr. Marvel patted her shoulder and then spoke briefly with Sergeant Courgette. A paramedic began packing up equipment. Courgette made a brief call on his cell phone before addressing the crowd. "Everyone, Dr. Marvel tells me Madame Johnston has died. The coroner and two of my officers will be here soon. Please do not leave until you give your name and contact information to my team."

Once Courgette's constables arrived, they set up interview stations at two empty tables. Slowly people formed orderly queues and waited patiently to share their information. Lacey and I tacked ourselves on to the end of the line in front of the female constable.

"I'm dry as the Sahara," Lacey said. "Do you have any water?"

"Over at the table."

Lacey glanced toward our Candystripers table, gasped and then took off at a run. Rosette stood in front of our table, her back to us. By the time I joined them, Lacey had grabbed Rosette's arm and spun her around, turning the fiery updo into a down-do.

"Stealing my pickles, Rosette? Planning to reverse engineer the recipe?"

Rosette smacked Lacey's hand away. "Don't touch me, you conniving rumourmonger. I never went near your pickles."

If Lacey had not caught Rosette stealing Tulip's pickle recipe two years ago, I would have discounted Lacey's concern as purely pickler's paranoia. However, Rosette *had* borrowed a recipe without permission. (You'll remember, Violet — I wrote an article for the Blossom City Gazette about it. *The Case of the Purloined Pickle*.)

Sergeant Courgette strolled over, his interest no doubt piqued by Lacey and Rosette's raised voices.

"What were you doing at our table, then?" I said to Rosette.

"Tidying up, hoping to avoid more spills." Rosette gestured at the spot where my pickles had fallen.

"Hah!" Lacey said. "Liar, liar, pants on fire. You want to resurrect your pickle business and need prize-winning recipes to do it."

Courgette cleared his throat. "Is that true?"

Rosette batted her eyelashes and patted her disheartened

coiffure. "No, Sergeant. I've enrolled in evening courses at the local college to reinvent myself."

I rolled my eyes at Lacey. We both knew Rosette's reinvention plan involved the digging of gold. She cozied up to every wealthy male she could corner before, during and after lectures.

"She was trying to steal my pickles," Lacey said, never one to let a paranoid thought get away.

"Your pickles aren't worth the jar they sit in," Rosette said. "Daisy herself said they missed the mark."

Lacey sneered. "Only because she needed a reason to declare her mother the winner again."

"You've hated Daisy ever since you lost the competition last year," Rosette said. "You wanted her dead."

Uh oh, I thought.

Sergeant Courgette said, "Pardon?"

Rosette smirked and said, "Not long before Daisy collapsed Lacey told me, 'The only way I'll have a chance of winning is if Daisy overdoses on pickles and dies.' And what do you know, Daisy died."

"Oh for heaven's sake, that was a joke," Lacey said.

Rosette snapped back, "Didn't sound like you were joking." She turned to Courgette. "She probably added some slow-acting poison to her pickles, so Daisy wouldn't die immediately after sampling one. That way none of us would suspect Lacey."

I said, "That's the most ridiculous thing you've ever said, Rosette. At one time or another Lacey has wished most of the townspeople dead, and they're all still alive. Except for poor Daisy, of course, but that's purely a coincidence."

Lacey whispered, "That's not helpful, Persie."

Courgette lifted Lacey's jar of pickles and held it to the light.

Lacey stood with her hands on her hips, chin jutted forward. "There's nothing in there but beets and brine."

Courgette squinted at the rosy-hued contents of the jar. "Hmmm."

To be honest, Violet, I really didn't like the sound of that "hmmm."

"There seems to be something at the bottom, seeds perhaps," Courgette said. "Or berries?"

"What?" Lacey reached for the jar. "Let me see."

Courgette held on to the jar. "Tut, tut, Madame. This is evidence. I must preserve the chain of custody."

The three of us, Lacey, Rosette and I, stood there, jaws dropped and eyes agoggle.

"Evidence?" I said.

"Mais oui. We have an unexplained death. We have an accusation of malice, certainly in desire and possibly in action. I must investigate thoroughly."

Courgette turned to face the crowd and raised his voice. "Attention." I winced at his pronunciation. Ah-ton-shee-un. Fingernails on a chalkboard.

When the crowd quieted, Courgette said, "We need samples of everything Madame Daisy ate or drank today. Please hand your pickles to an officer as evidence. Immédiatement." Another cringe-worthy nod to his non-existent French roots.

He turned to Rosette. "You assisted Daisy today?" At Rosette's nod, he said, "And that entailed?"

"Umm, handing her minted water and crackers as a palate cleanser, carrying paper napkins for her to wipe her fingers and lips."

"We need all of that."

Rosette paled. She pointed to the container by the side exit. "I dumped most of it."

Courgette called an officer over. "Retrieve all the water bottles, crackers and other food stuffs from the garbage. Put everything into evidence bags."

I tapped Sergeant Courgette's shoulder. "She also had mint leaves in her basket. For flavouring the, umm, water."

Courgette asked Rosette, "Are the leaves still in the basket?"

Rosette nodded.

"Bring it to me." Then Courgette focused on me. "Did you enter pickles in the contest, Persimmon? Where are they?"

"They spilled on the grass. I can put them back into the jar for you."

"Not you." He waved another constable over. "Madame Worthing will show you her spilled pickles. Please collect them."

I led the officer to where my once lovely, firm candy-stripe beets lay, now sad and limp. As he collected my pickles, I spotted a candy-stripe pickle remnant behind him. It bore the distinct imprint of Daisy's crooked front tooth. I was positive it was Lacey's, the one Daisy had tossed onto the table. (I know it was naughty of me, Violet, but I palmed it and when I had a chance slipped it into the phone pocket of my purse. *That* was a stupid move because by the time I got home and put the pickle into a plastic baggie in my fridge, the pickling brine smell had permeated my purse (my favourite gadding-about-town purse which now has been banished to the garden shed.)

I digress.

The police gathered their evidence. Courgette told everyone not to leave town without checking with him first. "Especially you," he said to Lacey.

Nine days later the police arrested Lacey on suspicion of murder. Courgette confided in me the forensic lab discovered belladonna berries in her pickle jar. He revealed Daisy had died from heart failure, probably caused by exposure to a toxin. "I think they will find it was a belladonna extract," he said.

The next morning I posted a surety for Lacey. The staff at the Blossom City jail cheered when I showed up with the order for her release.

The supervisor took me aside. "I appreciate your generosity. The moment Lacey arrived, my staff began second-guessing their career choice. She called their uniforms 'clothes for the downtrodden, made by a malevolent sadist.' She offered to repaint the cells 'in something other than this babyshit brown.' She called the cafeteria 'Upchuck Cantina.' All that in her first hour of residency. And not one of my night staff had a moment's peace because her snores kept every other inmate awake and threatening to riot."

Lacey was fitted with an ankle bracelet and released into my custody. That evening we sat at my kitchen table, drinking Taylor's Tawny Port and assessing the case against her: She and Daisy had a fractious history; Lacey resented Daisy awarding the Pickle Jar to her mother last year; Lacey voiced a wish that Daisy would die; belladonna berries were found in Lacey's pickles; Daisy died from complications after ingesting a toxin.

"But I didn't do it," Lacey said. She covered her face with her hands. "I'm going to jail. An innocent woman, spending the rest of her life behind bars for a crime she didn't commit. You can't imagine what it's like in jail, Persie. The décor, the food, the wardrobe, it all screams government-run."

"I can recommend a good lawyer," I said.

"Omigod! Legal fees! I'll have to write a memoir just to pay them."

"Let's hope it doesn't come to that," I said, not at all confident memoir sales would be sufficient to fund a trip to Tofino, never mind pay for a defence against a murder charge.

I spent a sleepless night. The next morning I rose determined to solve Daisy's murder, if only to ensure Lacey could move out of my spare room and take her snores with her.

I rooted through my fridge for the baggie containing Lacey's half-eaten pickle from the contest. Then I invited Sergeant Courgette to join me for a mid-morning break at La Patisserie. I arrived at the café well before him and spoke with the owner. When Courgette appeared, my table in the coziest corner of the café held a large French press of coffee and a selection of his favourite treats: pain au chocolat, mille-feuille, crème brûlée, and a large slice of gâteau St. Honoré.

I idly pushed the crumbs of a croissant around my plate as Courgette settled into the seat across the table.

I poured coffee into his cup. "You must have these pastries."

He gazed at the spread, sighed and shook his head. "You know we officers of the peace cannot accept gifts."

"I wouldn't call this a gift from me to you. In fact, you'd be giving me the gift."

"Oh?" The glimmer of hope lit his eyes.

"My eyes are bigger than my stomach. It's a failing. I hate to waste them. You'd be doing a good deed for me."

Courgette wriggled in his chair, settling in. "Yes, I see. When you put it like that, I'd be honoured to help."

He reached for the St. Honoré cake and then pulled his hand back. "No. The best, last."

His spoon pierced the crust of the crème brûlée with a smack. When he put the first spoonful of custard and brûlée topping into his mouth, I said, "How is your investigation into Daisy's death going, Milton? Have you discovered anything besides belladonna berries?"

He shook his head and wiped his mouth with his napkin. "All the other pickle samples were pristine. No deleterious substances in any of them." He paused and then offered a small smile. "We did discover one interesting thing."

"Oh really?"

"Yes. Daisy's minted water was not water at all. It was a combination of club soda, rum, mint and basil. Her blood alcohol at the time of her death was over the limit."

"Basil?" I said. "In her drink?"

"Yes." He pulled the mille-feuille over to his side of the table.

"Did you find basil anywhere else in the tent?" I said.

He lifted a large forkful of mille-feuille toward his mouth and nodded. "I believe there was Thai basil, as well as mint, in Rosette's basket."

"Really?"

He swallowed. "However, we tested both Daisy's drink and the basket contents and none of them contained a poison."

I leaned forward, pushing the pain au chocolat over to him. "Did you know Daisy was terribly allergic to basil?"

He bit into the pastry, chewed and then wiped a touch of chocolate away from the corner of his mouth. "Errrrr, no."

"She was. It made Daisy's heart race and constricted her lungs." I shook my head. "This has me so confused. Of the two of us, Milton, you are the brainy one."

He preened and swallowed the last bite of his pain au chocolat.

I said, "Why would she put basil into her mojito when she had such a severe allergy?"

He reached for the pièce de résistance, the St. Honoré cake. I poured more coffee into his cup. He took a bite of the pastry and raised his eyes heavenward. Eventually he said, "She would not put that substance into her drink if it caused heart issues."

"Oh! Then, are you saying someone else put the basil in the drink?"

He nodded slowly. "Possibly. By accident?"

"Perhaps. Mint leaves and Thai basil leaves look very similar."

He relaxed against the back of his chair. "There you go, then."

"Allow me to put a devious spin on things for a moment," I said. "Hypothetically, suppose someone wanted to slip basil into

Daisy's drink. Wouldn't that be a superb way to do it? Hide it among mint leaves?"

"Yes, that would work. Hypothetically." He took another bite of the St. Honoré and shrugged. "But Lacey wished Daisy dead. She bore a grudge because of last year's competition. She had a definite motive."

I considered who else might want to kill Daisy and came up with two people. I leaned toward him and whispered, "You know I *never* gossip. But in the service of justice, I feel I must break that rule and share a few tidbits."

He lifted another forkful of St. Honoré to his mouth. "It is your civic duty."

"I heard Ashley Jones' lover was Basil Phickle and that he jilted her in favour of Daisy. People say Ashley hated Daisy ever since then."

Courgette laughed. "A woman scorned is a cliché, Persimmon. An outdated solution."

"Forgive me. I'm such a novice at crime-solving."

He waved my faux apology away.

"Luckily," I said, "you are much too good at your job to discount a motive because it sounds like a cliché."

He inclined his head graciously. I went on. "Also, did you know Daisy disqualified Rosette two years ago when she stole a pickle recipe from Tulip? The disqualification cost Rosette her business."

"Hmmm."

"Could Ashley or Rosette be a suspect?"

He finished the St. Honoré, drained his coffee and sat back. "They could have motives, yes. Rosette would make a solid suspect since she handled Daisy's drink."

I said, "My devious side thinks Ashley could have spiked the drink. I suppose your lab could check the bottle for her fingerprints?"

He nodded.

At last, we were getting somewhere. I wouldn't have to confess to pocketing what could be evidence. Lacey would be back in her own home in short order. I would be able to sleep through the night.

But then Courgette shook his head. "No. Here is a lesson in crime solving, Persimmon — the obvious answer is the best one. Daisy may have been allergic to basil, but the real culprit will be the belladonna, which Lacey put into her pickles."

I sighed. If I went to jail, so be it. At least I might get a night's sleep. I reached into my purse, removed the plastic baggie and placed it on the table. Courgette stared at the baggie with its lone candy-stripe pickle bearing the imprint of Daisy's crooked tooth.

"This is Lacey's pickle that Daisy tasted," I said.

Courgette's eyes widened. "Stealing evidence, Persimmon?"

"I prefer to say preserving evidence. Besides, I didn't know it was evidence at the time." He didn't answer so I went on, "Would a lab be able to compare that bite impression with her teeth? And test the pickle for belladonna?"

The look he gave me reminded me of all the times I disappointed my mother. But he pocketed the baggie.

I endured two more nights of Lacey's snoring before Courgette phoned me with an update. "You were correct. The lab found no trace of belladonna on the pickle you gave me. Of course, the chain of custody on that vital piece of evidence is non-existent. It's fortunate you are trustworthy."

"Why thank you, Milton."

"Plus you are nowhere near brilliant enough to cook the books, so to speak."

"Yes, thanks for that, too. Where will you go from here?"

"I have made progress. Ashley, the jilted lover, is in the clear.

Her fingerprints are not on either of Daisy's drink bottles."

"Oh."

"As I said, Persimmon, your suspicion of her was nothing more than a cliché."

I gritted my teeth.

Courgette continued. "Rosette, however, is another story. We will lay charges against her soon and then we can relieve Lacey of her ankle bracelet."

And I could have a nap. "Rosette confessed?"

"Au contraire."

"But she put the berries into Lacey's pickle jar?"

"Denies it."

"Well, your crackerjack lab can prove her wrong. Her fingerprints must be on the jar?"

"No."

That threw me. Lacey caught Rosette stealing Tulip Johnston's recipe and reported her to Daisy, who disqualified her. Rosette blamed both of them for the nosedive her pickle business took. If Rosette poisoned Daisy and wanted to blame the other person she hated, it made sense she would be the one who put the berries into Lacey's pickles. But apparently not.

I cast my mind back to that day in the tent. I contemplated who else might have a grudge against both Daisy and Lacey. I thought about belladonna. And then, Violet, I had the obvious answer (no doubt that would please Courgette).

To convince him to play along with my plan I played the novice card once more. "Milton, I'm such a know-nothing when it comes to investigations, could I ask you to help me?"

A few hours later Courgette accompanied me to the Golden Times Homestead. I pointed out a ground floor window with a hummingbird feeder hanging from the overhead ledge.

"That must be her window. Crouch beneath it and I'll open it so you can listen in."

He balked. "Persimmon, I went along with you and sent my evidence team to Daisy's house to collect her food stuffs. The lab is re-testing the pickle jar and water bottles. But here I draw the line. I am a Sergeant of the Blossom City Police. Sergeants do not crouch beneath windows."

"I'm only thinking of your reputation, Milton. Suppose I bungle my little interview through inexperience and you are right there with me? Everyone will blame you for the debacle. But if you are outside the window you can protect yourself from embarrassment yet still hear the conversation."

"Errrrr, yes. When you put it that way, it seems reasonable."

"Fine. Now, one thing? If you touch the leaves or berries of that plant under her window, *do not* lick your fingers. That's a very well-tended belladonna."

"Are you sure?"

"Positive. You might know criminals, but I know plants and that definitely is belladonna."

He paled and rubbed his hand over the back of his neck. "Merde."

This time he nailed the pronunciation.

Once Courgette was in place, I entered the seniors' residence and knocked on Tulip's door. When she answered, I held up the box of Timbits and the two take-out teas I'd brought along. "You must be wretchedly lonely without Daisy. I thought we could share gardening or pickling secrets. Or both."

She stammered and stuttered but I breezed past her into the studio apartment and put my offerings on the coffee table, next to a potted plant. Tulip followed me and plopped into a claret-coloured armchair (which did nothing for her orange sweat suit, I might say). I handed her a tea and the doughnuts.

I turned a tight circle in the living room. "How cozy.

Everything within arm's reach." I fanned my face. "It's a bit warm, though."

I opened the window. Sergeant Courgette crouched beneath it, staring at the belladonna as if it would wrap its branches around him at any moment.

I claimed a chair across from Tulip. "Did Daisy help you choose this studio?"

Tulip plucked a Timbit from the box. "*She* chose it. Apparently she worried about me falling in my house or garden and said I would be safer here. I suppose I am. Bored to death but safe."

"Hmm. Too bad she couldn't move into the house with you."

Tulip nodded and sighed. "I suggested that. But she poo-pooed it, said the house was only big enough for one."

I played with the lid on my tea. "I have a confession to make."

She stiffened.

I leaned forward. "There's an ulterior motive for my visit. I hope you'll share your recipe for mojitos. Daisy seemed buoyed by the ones you made for the pickle competition. Mine are humdrum. What's your secret?"

Tulip shook her head. "Daisy drank minted water during the competition."

I chuckled. "That's not true. Her drink spilled beside me. I definitely smelled rum."

"Really? I didn't know she had a mojito in the bottle."

I smiled. "Of course you did. When I saw you in the liquor store you were buying the ingredients to make her mojitos."

She shook her head. "I made mojitos for her now and then but I don't remember doing it for the competition."

I waved her comment away. "Whatever. I'm more interested in your recipe."

"It's the standard ratio of white rum to soda and some crushed mint."

I fingered the leaves of the plant on her coffee table. "And your secret ingredient, the one that gives the mojito an extra punch?"

"A squeeze of lemon and a teaspoon of sugar," she said.

"This is a lovely specimen," I said, still touching the plant. "Thai basil. It's remarkable how similar its leaves are to mint."

She stared at the herb. "I hadn't realized that until you pointed it out."

I nodded. "I'm sure. The police found Thai basil in Daisy's mojito."

"No! Someone slipped it into the bottle?"

I nodded. "Whoever made those mojitos added mint *and* Thai basil. That's your secret ingredient, isn't it?"

Tulip snorted. "I wouldn't put basil into a mojito. Anyway I never made the drink for her that day."

"You must have. Your fingerprints are all over those bottles. Rosette claims you gave the drinks to her for Daisy."

She stared at me, mouth opening and closing like a hungry koi. "That fake redhead is a liar. *She* probably put the basil into the drink."

I shook my head. "She said you also gave her extra mint leaves for the drinks. She didn't even know there was basil mixed in with the mint. If there's one thing Rosette is not, it's a gardener."

"I'll tell you what she is. A thief. She stole my pickle recipe. I made Daisy ban her from the competition and now she's trying to get even by accusing me."

"Rosette didn't know Daisy was allergic to basil. Passed a lie detector test just this morning." I doubted Blossom City's police department had a lie detector machine, but by the look on Tulip's face she believed they did.

She changed tack. "Okay. I put a tiny bit of basil into the mojito. There are studies now saying if you ingest small amounts of an allergen, you build up resistance and eventually are cured."

She nodded as if to convince herself. "Yes. My only goal was to cure Daisy and help her live a better life. But her life was snatched away by your friend Lacey Lavender."

"Somebody certainly wanted to make it look that way." I glanced at her window. "Well, isn't that marvelous! Probably the last remaining belladonna plant in all of Blossom City is right outside your window. Its flowers are beautiful, aren't they?"

"Oh?" Tulip said. "I hadn't noticed it."

I shook my head and chuckled. "You're having me on. I'm merely a novice gardener and I knew what it was. You're a master gardener so I'm sure you'd recognize it instantly. And it's taller than your windowsill. You can see it simply by glancing out your window."

She smiled. "You're very astute, Persimmon. Yes, I was pulling your leg. I keep that plant a secret because it's the one bright spot in this horrid apartment." She sighed and looked around her studio. "At least now that Daisy's gone I can move back home. Get away from this . . . this tomb."

"Handy to have belladonna berries right outside your window. When did you decide to put them into Lacey's pickles?"

"What? I never did! Lacey added the berries."

"Nope. The police tested Lacey's pickle that Daisy sampled. It was merely a beet pickle. No belladonna at all."

"Well then, Rosette did it. Yes, that makes sense. Lacey reported Rosette for stealing my recipe. Rosette would want to get even with her too."

I shook my head again. "There was a very short time between Daisy tasting Lacey's pickle and your visiting me at our table. Remember jostling things and fussing about putting the lid on Lacey's jar? Rosette was nowhere near Lacey's pickles then. But you were. You distracted us with patter about spilled pickles and dumped the berries into the jar just before you replaced the lid."

"That's ridiculous. Rosette probably returned to the table and added the berries later."

"If so her fingerprints would be on the jar. Instead of just Lacey's and yours. Was it payback because Lacey accused you of adding food colouring to your pickles last year?"

Tulip threw back her head and laughed. "That's rich! I have much better things to do than worry about snoops and troublemakers like Lacey." She drained her tea. "I've had enough of your accusations. You can't save Lacey's scrawny neck by putting the blame on me."

I stood and raised my voice, delivering the cue Courgette needed. "Fine. I shall take my Timbits and leave."

Five seconds later, as planned, my cell phone rang. I answered and listened, inserting "uh-huh," and "oh, really?" where I thought fitting. Then I said, "Thanks for the update, Sergeant," and ended the call.

Tulip was halfway to the door in her sensible shoes (no doubt dying to wish me goodbye) when I said, "Most interesting. I'd buy a plane ticket out of here if I were you."

She stopped and returned to where I lingered near her window. "Pardon?"

"That was Sergeant Courgette. He is *very* skilled. He said they have seized all the teas, coffee and seasonings from Daisy's home. Also the stew in her fridge. Which apparently was her last meal before she died."

"Oh?" Tulip sat down.

"He also said test results show Daisy had extremely high concentrations of basil in her body. Her heart and other organs showed signs of damage from prolonged exposure to allergens. I'm sure they'll find basil in everything they seized. You weren't trying to cure her. You were slowly killing her, weren't you?"

"That's ridiculous."

I shrugged. "As I said, I'd think about leaving town, because the police have a witness who will put you in jail for a long time."

She went pale and put her hand to her throat. "What? Who?"

I offered a silent prayer to the heavens that Tulip's memory would be fuzzy. "Someone who months ago heard you tell Daisy you wanted to move back to the house. And then heard Daisy say, 'over my dead body.'"

Tulip sat silently, clenching and unclenching her fists.

"That's all you wanted, isn't it?" I said. "To move back home?"

Tears ran down Tulip's cheeks. "It was my house. My home, my garden. She booted me out, cast me adrift. She made me run her errands and cook her casseroles just so I could have the *honour* of spending an hour in the house."

"So you began slipping basil into her food. Knowing what it did to her heart and lungs."

Tulip sighed. "She was supposed to die in her sleep long before now. But she didn't. And then the pickle competition came along. She said I didn't deserve to win this year, that anyone who would add food colouring to the brine was not a true 'artiste.' So I laced the stew with basil. Mounds of it."

She straightened her shoulders and smiled. "The day of the competition she was still alive but having heart palpitations. I realized if she died during the contest I could kill three birds with one stone. I could spike the drink and make Rosette look guilty, I could add belladonna to Lacey's pickles and make her look guilty and I could move back into my house once Daisy died. Unfortunately I couldn't get near Lacey's pickles before Daisy tasted them. Otherwise, the plan would have been flawless."

Tulip shrugged. "If Daisy had somehow survived, I would have kept on spiking her food. Eventually she would have succumbed."

She stood and grinned at me. "Now, I have a plane to catch. And by the way, you can't prove a thing. I'll deny everything."

Courgette popped up outside her window. "Tulip Johnston, you are under arrest for murder."

Tulip shoved me backward. Her sensible-shoe-shuffle disappeared the very next instant and she sprinted for the door. By the time I reached it, she was a blur of orange halfway down the hall. If orthopedic shoes could lay rubber, you'd have noticed the smell. Courgette stepped into the hallway from the Homestead's lobby and enveloped Tulip in his arms. "As I said, Madame, you are under arrest."

Reality really is stranger than fiction, isn't it, Violet? Perhaps we should have anticipated this whole affair because it followed the usual pattern of happenings in Blossom City — petty misdemeanors like recipe theft, food colouring fraud, and reverse nepotism building on each other like the waves along the breakwater protecting our marina, to end the reign of the Judge of Blossom City's renowned Perfect Pickle Competition. Daisy's death is the culmination of another typical Blossom City crime wave.

It's a shame Daisy's dead. The Perfect Pickle Competition committee is in a tizzy. It's such a challenge to find someone with the palate necessary to taste-test pickles. Between you and me, Daisy had a peck of faults — perhaps a bushel — but I'll give her this: her pickle palate was beyond compare.

I'm glad Lacey won't spend the rest of her days in prison. Can you imagine her in prison? I shudder when I think of the devastation. Fortunately the Canadian penal system is intact.

I'll write again soon, Violet. Unless, of course, Sergeant Courgette is befuddled by another of our town's crime sprees.

Your loving aunt,
Persimmon

ACKNOWLEDGMENTS

It takes a village to bring an anthology to life.

Sisters in Crime — Canada West thanks our very own village: our Past President, Linda L. Richards, whose idea it was to publish a collection of members' stories; the anthology committee (Karen L. Abrahamson, Jayne Barnard, Merrilee Robson, Marcelle Dubé and Michelle Cornish) who bravely volunteered to shepherd the anthology from dream to published book; the many wonderful members of our chapter who produced excellent short stories and made the selection decisions extremely difficult for the committee; the editors (Karen L. Abrahamson and Jayne Barnard) who collaborated with the authors of the selected stories and helped turn already fine stories into jewels; the copy editors and proofreaders who undertook a relentless hunt for typos and glitches; our designers (Michelle Cornish for the cover, and Marcelle Dubé and Karen L. Abrahamson for the interior); and Sisters in Crime Inc., without whose guidance and support our chapter and this anthology would not exist.

And most of all, we thank you for reading the anthology —

the stories were written with your enjoyment in mind and we sincerely hope you enjoy the collection and want to come back for more.

AUTHOR BIOGRAPHIES

Called the "Queen of Comedy" by the Toronto Sun, and the "Canadian literary heir to Donald Westlake" by EQMM, Vancouver-raised crime writer **Melodie Campbell** has connections in low places, as evidenced by The Goddaughter mob caper series. Melodie has shared a literary shortlist with Margaret Atwood, and was seen lurking on the Amazon Top 50 Bestseller list between Tom Clancy and Nora Roberts. Her sixteen novels and fifty short stories have won ten awards, including the Derringer and the Arthur Ellis. She didn't even steal them. Melodie is the former Executive Director of Crime Writers of Canada.

K.L. Abrahamson writes mystery, fantasy and romance and sometimes a blend of all three. Her short story, "With One Shoe," was a finalist for the Crime Writers of Canada Arthur Ellis award for best crime short story. Her historical novella, *Death by Effigy* (Guardbridge Books) blends mystery and fantasy. Her alternate history mystery series, the Detective Kazakov Mysteries, were released in 2018 and 2019. Writing as K.L. Abrahamson, Karen draws on her background in the criminal justice system to craft police procedurals as well as short stories and novels about amateur and women sleuths. She lives on the coast of British Columbia with bears, bald eagles and orcas for neighbours.

J.E. (Jayne) Barnard is best known for the Maddie Hatter Adventures (Tyche), and now The Falls Mysteries (Dundurn). Her works have won the Dundurn Unhanged Arthur, the Alberta Book of the Year, the Bony Pete and the Saskatchewan Writers Guild Award, and were shortlisted for the Prix Aurora, the UK Debut Dagger, the Book Publishing Alberta Award (BPAA) and three times for the Great Canadian Story prize. Her most recent novel is *Where the Ice Falls*, a ghostly tale of three women's struggles to succeed in the macho Alberta foothills.

Alice Bienia is a Calgary novelist and short story author. Her first novel, *Knight Blind,* was a finalist for the Arthur Ellis award for Best Unpublished Crime Manuscript. Her short fiction is published in *The Dame Was Trouble*, an anthology featuring some of the best female crime writers of Canada. A former geologist, her work in remote regions of Canada honed her passion for adventure, reading, storytelling, coffee and all things absurd and sublime. When not plotting a murder, Alice amuses herself watching foreign flicks and exploring Calgary's urban parks and pathways.

Marcelle Dubé writes mystery, science fiction and fantasy. Sometimes at the same time. She is best known for the Mendenhall Mystery series, which is set in the fictional town of Mendenhall, Manitoba and features Chief of Police Kate Williams, "a heroine for our times," as one reviewer named her. Her most recent novel is *Epidemic: An A'lle Chronicles Mystery*, which is set in Lower Canada. It is alternate history, science fiction and mystery and is the second in her A'lle Chronicles mysteries.

Debra Henry, a retired anthropologist and educator, is an award-winning author who's published several short stories in literary journals, including *Island Writer*. "Local Intelligence" introduces Turnaround Bay, the setting of Debra's upcoming novel, *Hooked on Murder*, in which constables Hazel Quinn and Mark Connors investigate the brutal killing of a fish farm employee. When not writing, Debra participates in triathlons and enjoys travelling the world from her home on Canada's west coast in Victoria, BC.

Winona Kent is the author of seven novels: two tongue-in-cheek spy stories, *Skywatcher* and *The Cilla Rose Affair*; three accidental time-travel/historical romances, *Persistence of Memory*, *In Loving Memory* and *Marianne's Memory*; and two mysteries featuring professional musician/amateur sleuth Jason Davey, *Cold Play* and her latest, *Notes on a Missing G-String*, which was published by Blue Devil Books in August 2019. Jason also featured in Winona's 2017 novella, *Disturbing the Peace*.

Winona recently retired from her job at UBC and moved to New Westminster, where she's thoroughly enjoying being a full-time writer.

Charlotte Morganti has been a burger flipper, beer slinger and a corporate finance/mining lawyer. In addition to her law degree, she holds a Master of Fine Arts in creative writing. Now retired from legal practice, she focuses on writing crime fiction novels and short stories, ranging from gritty investigations to lighter capers. Her novels have been short-listed for various awards (including the Crime Writers of Canada Unhanged Arthur award) and her short stories have appeared in several anthologies. She and her husband live on the Sunshine Coast of British Columbia.

A servant to two cats, **Merrilee Robson** uses the time when the cats are sleeping to write mysteries. Fortunately, cats sleep a lot. Her first novel, *Murder is Uncooperative*, is set in a Vancouver housing co-op. Her short stories have appeared in *Ellery Queen*

Mystery Magazine, The People's Friend, Malice Domestic 15, Over My Dead Body, Mysteryrat's Maze Podcast, Flare, and other publications. She lives in Vancouver with her husband and the cats.

"Autumn is a Time for Dying" is inspired by her grandfather's time as a RNWP and RCMP officer.

Manufactured by Amazon.ca
Bolton, ON